THE CASE OF THE COPPER KING

A *McKenzie Sisters* MYSTERY NOVEL

MK McCLINTOCK

Published by Trappers Peak Publishing
Bigfork, Montana 59911
www.mkmcclintock.com

Publisher's Note: This is a work of fiction. Names, characters, places, and incidents are a product of the author's imagination or are used fictitiously. Locales and public names are sometimes used for fictitious and atmospheric purposes. Any resemblance to actual people, living or dead, or to businesses, companies, events, institutions, or locales is entirely coincidental.

The Case of the Copper King; novel/MK McClintock
ISBN: 978-1737758884 (hardcover)

Cover Design by MK McClintock
Cover Background © TeriVirbickis | Deposit Photos
Woman in Dress | Shutterstock

PRAISE FOR THE WRITINGS OF

MK McCLINTOCK

"An absolutely delightful mystery adventure that will keep you guessing till the last chapter! *The Case of the Copper King* is a must-read if you love western mysteries with a touch of romance and lots of twists and turns." —*Nicole Laverdure, 5 Stars*

"Ms. McClintock's stories are adventurous and full of budding romance that transports you back to a simpler time where the outside world ceases to exist once you open one of her books."
—*My Life, One Story at a Time*

"Wow! What a series. I guarantee you won't be able to stop reading. Well done MK!"
—*Pioneer Hearts Reader* on The Montana Gallagher series

"Ms. McClintock succeeds in masterfully weaving both genres meticulously together until mystery lovers are sold on romance and romance lovers love the mystery!"
—InD'Tale Magazine on *Alaina Claiborne*

"*Journey to Hawk's Peak* by MK McClintock is one of the most gripping and thrilling western novels that anyone will ever read. This is probably the best novel that I have yet read as a reviewer. It clicks on all cylinders—grammar, punctuation, plot, characterization, everything. This novel is a serious page-turner, and for fans of western fiction, it is a must-read." —*Readers' Favorite*

THE MONTANA GALLAGHER SERIES

Gallagher's Pride

Gallagher's Hope

Gallagher's Choice

An Angel Called Gallagher

Journey to Hawk's Peak

Wild Montana Winds

The Healer of Briarwood

McKENZIE SISTERS MYSTERY SERIES

The Case of the Copper King

BRITISH AGENT SERIES

Alaina Claiborne

Blackwood Crossing

Clayton's Honor

SHORT STORY COLLECTIONS

A Home for Christmas

The Women of Crooked Creek

Discover all of MK's writings at mkmcclintock.com.

To Abe, who threw me off the saddle during a wild run in the Colorado mountains and who taught me to always get back up on the horse.

CHAPTER 1

Colorado Springs, Colorado 1899

As one of five women making the rounds in the Lone Dog Saloon, the proprietor expected her to be in high demand. The silky blond hair was pulled up to frame her face while the rest flowed around her shoulders. She drew the attention of every man she passed at the tables, offering a wink, smile, or small wave to each of them.

None of them held her interest.

She sidled up to one man and held a half-full bottle close to her chest.

"Care for a drink, cowboy?"

"I like a little sugar with my whiskey."

"Sugar is extra, sweetheart."

"How much extra?"

Amber liquid fell from the bottle into the shot glass on the scarred bar. "Ten dollars."

"That's mighty steep for a place like this, darlin'."

Her fingers trailed up his dusty vest. "I'm worth it, *darlin'*."

His boisterous laugh startled a few of the patrons. "Where's your room?"

"Not so fast. I like to know the names of the men I take to my bed."

"Name's Fletcher. I ain't gonna take you to bed, darlin'. I'm gonna take you to heaven."

Casey palmed the Deringer and pressed it against her quarry's belly. "Fletcher Jones. You've been a hard man to find."

Fletcher's smile vanished as he looked at her with cold, hard eyes. "You got me mixed up with someone else."

"I don't think so."

"You ain't got what it takes to pull the trigger."

"I've heard a lot of things about you, Fletcher. Not all accounts agree on what you look like, who you ride with, or how many innocent people you've killed, but they agree on one thing."

He smirked. "What's that?"

"You're a very stupid man." She pressed the pistol harder against his gut. "No, no, stay right there. Don't make this worse for yourself. I want an audience, but I'm guessing you don't. Where is your partner?"

Fletcher leaned close, the whiskey on his breath pungent and unpleasant. "Who are you?"

Casey smiled. "The person tired of hunting you."

"Bounty hunter." Fletcher spat the words.

"You're not that lucky, Fletcher. Any time now, Sheriff."

Fletcher whirled around too fast, and Casey was standing too close. He pushed away from the bar only to be met by Sheriff Crankshaw's fist in his face. Fletcher reeled back and knocked into Casey.

Strong arms and a firm grip caught her mid-stumble, saving her from an undignified landing on her backside. Grateful she did not have to climb up from the floor with the corset strangling what was left of her oxygen, Casey set herself aright. "Sheriff—"

Fletcher yanked her close. "Ain't no whore is takin' me down."

"Oh, I'm much worse than a whore." Casey pulled out of his grasp. "You have five seconds to tell me where to find your partner."

"Or what?"

"Four seconds."

Sheriff Crankshaw wrestled Fletcher's arms behind his back and secured them with shackles.

"Time is up, Fletcher." Casey leaned on the bar, then immediately stood straight. The corset dug into her flesh every time she tried to defy ramrod-straight posture. "I will find your partner, just like I found you. Now you can spend the rest of your miserable life cutting big rocks down to little ones." She said to the sheriff, "He's all yours."

"Wait!"

A hush had fallen over the saloon. Even the entertainer with the mousy brown hair and voice like a lark stood quietly beside the piano, waiting to see what would happen next.

"Do you have something to say, Fletcher?" Casey dared to move a little closer. "I know all about how you threaten folks in the towns you pass through to pay you for protection. You forget to tell them the only person they need protection from is you. These folks will not be sorry to see you go. The sheriff might be able to keep you safe long enough to be transferred . . . or maybe not. I suppose it depends on how liquored up these fine people get."

Fletcher looked over the room. "Who are you, lady?"

"Someone, who, with any luck, will never have to see you again." Casey rolled her shoulders against the stiffness in her back. She needed to get out of the dress. "Your partner, Fletcher. Who is he?"

"What's in it for me?"

"I might be convinced to talk Sheriff Crankshaw here into loading you on the train bound for Denver or St. Louis. You can stand trial where no one knows you," Casey pointed to the room, "or take your chances here."

Fletcher grumbled, swore a few times, and said, "Deke's gone to El Paso."

"That wasn't so hard, now, was it?"

Sheriff Crankshaw jerked Fletcher into moving toward the door. He dug his boots into the wooden floorboards as the voices and music picked up again. He turned to Casey and said, "Ain't no one's come close in three years. Who are you?"

Casey crossed the short distance, sensing everyone watching her. She stopped a foot away, and in a voice too low to carry, said, "No one you'll ever see again."

CHAPTER 2

Casey McKenzie stared back at the semi-familiar reflection and removed the glorious blond locks. The edges of her scalp itched from having worn the wig for too long. She massaged her fingers through her hair as she removed the pins holding the light auburn curls in place.

When she next attempted to untie the corset herself, she debated for about ten seconds between finding the maid who had helped her into it or tearing it off. She settled for running a knife carefully through the laces, exhaling deeply every time one of the laces popped free.

"Only a man could think such a contraption was worth inventing." She did not know if it was a man but would wager her sister, Rose, knew. The errant thought reminded Casey that she owed Rose a telegram, or better yet, a letter. It had been a week since her last communication, and Rose had been thoughtful enough to send her one. Or had it been two weeks? She sent it from the telegraph office in Cheyenne . . . "Three weeks." She decided a visit to Denver was in order. She had some free time coming and could use a decent bath. Casey thought of the oversized porcelain tub in her room at the Denver house, complete with hot and cold running water. Casey appreciated a luxurious bath.

She stood in a thin chemise, stockings, and fancy boots that pinched her heels when there was a knock at the door. The corset had prevented her from bending over far enough to remove those first. "Who is it?"

"Sheriff Crankshaw."

"I'm off duty now, Sheriff."

"I've been asked to fetch you, Detecti—err, Miss McKenzie."

Casey's robe hung on the back of the closet door. She realized a maid had been in there sometime during the evening. "Just a minute." She took down the robe, slipped her arms into the sleeves, and pulled the edges together so one overlapped the other as far as it would go.

She opened the door a few inches and peered around the side, while keeping her body hidden. "It's late, Sheriff."

"Mr. Johnson asked me to give you this note."

Casey accepted the missive, broke her supervisor's pretentious seal, and read the two sentences. She glanced at the bed with longing and released a sigh. "Tell Mr. Johnson I will be along directly."

Twenty-five minutes later, Casey walked into the railroad station restaurant. Only one other lone occupant sat in the small dining room, his clothes incongruous to the setting, as were hers.

He sat against the opposite wall near a window, close to the entrance. She gave him and the two waiters no mind and crossed to the table against the back wall. Mr. Johnson had not been active in the field for five years, a fact attested to by his growing midsection on display when he stood at Casey's approach.

"You have done well, Detective McKenzie."

Casey sat in the chair he pulled out for her. An easier feat without the corset. The stifling dress with all the ruffles and deep décolletage would soon have a new home with one of the saloon's full-time girls. For meetings like this, where she wished to go unnoticed, Casey much preferred the white cotton blouse that buttoned to her neck, the well-worn leather vest, and her favorite split skirt. The tan duster she wore was both for comfort and practical purposes, one of which was to conceal her shape—and the pistol she carried at her hip.

"I prefer not to be referred to as 'Detective' while in the field, sir."

Johnson smoothed a finger over the edges of his mustache. "An oddity that. When you were transferred under my charge for this assignment, I was warned you had different methods. I did not believe you were right for this case, but you have done what no other member of law enforcement has done in three years."

"The others who have chased him had a distinct disadvantage."

"Those are highly skilled men to which you refer, Miss

McKenzie."

"*Men* being the operative problem. Fletcher Jones is not as stupid as people think—except when it comes to women. It was always going to take a woman to bring him down."

"You made the same argument when you requested this case. If memory serves, and it always does, prostitution is prohibited in Colorado Springs, Miss McKenzie."

She wondered how much her hand would hurt if she hit Johnson's arrogant jaw. "It helps when the current sheriff looks the other way. The job got done."

"Yes, it did, and a success for you is a success for the agency."

Casey nodded, weary now of Johnson's invasion into her evening. She doubted he would ever fully accept women as a permanent part of what he considered a man's agency. Never mind that Pinkerton women had been foiling the plans of criminals ever since Kate Warne convinced Allan Pinkerton of her undeniable value.

"The job isn't over until Fletcher's partner is brought in." Casey thanked the waiter who brought a tea service to the table, apparently ordered before her arrival. "Fletcher said Deke is in El Paso, which means he's probably in the opposite direction. The only Deke I know of who has ridden with Fletcher is Deke Ballow."

"As I said, you have done very well. Fletcher Jones has eluded capture for too long and now will be brought to justice, but the case is over for you."

Casey held her teacup in midair. "I don't understand. After my leave, I planned to finish the job and catch Ballow. Give him a week or two and he'll think we've given up."

"There is a more urgent matter, and it is has been agreed that your unique skill set is what the client needs."

The cup rattled a little in the saucer when Casey set it down. She believed her precious few days off, an uneventful trip to Denver, and a few hours spent in the big, beautiful tub were about to be taken away. Casey loved what she did, but there was the occasional moment when she asked herself why she bothered with the rules, restrictions, and growing distrust from the public.

"Who is this client?"

Mr. Johnson slid an envelope across the table, his eyes looking left, then right, before releasing it. He enjoyed dramatics. Casey stopped herself from sighing and instead picked up the envelope. She carefully removed the document, unfolded it, and read her assignment.

"With all due respect, sir, is this a joke?"

CHAPTER 3

"If you do not feel you are up to the challenge, Miss—"

"I am not confused by the challenge, sir, it is the client. I was guaranteed cases of my choosing, and I choose to help those who *need* help. Finding stolen money for wealthy men bent on destroying the land does not qualify."

Johnson adjusted his hefty body in the chair. "You are employed by the Pinkerton Agency, are you not?"

Casey imagined that Kate Warne, Allan Pinkerton's right-hand female detective, would not tolerate as much as Casey seemed to be right now. "I am, Mr. Johnson, though it is not binding employment, and I still have my agreement on the cases I select. I was also guaranteed time off after this last assignment. I'm on the train to Denver in the morning."

"Come now. What're a few more days to resolve this, keep the clients happy, and in turn, might I add, keep the agency happy?"

It was not the case, Casey admitted to herself, for it sounded simple enough compared to the last one. She objected to the interference with her plans . . . plans she had looked forward to with increasing enthusiasm, which surprised her. She enjoyed riding the rails and embarking on one adventure after another, and she especially relished seeing criminals get their comeuppance.

For reasons she had yet to determine, she needed a break from the constant moving about. Or was it the orders she'd grown weary of following?

Johnson interrupted her mulling. "Would it make a difference to learn a man was killed in the course of this robbery?" Casey despised Johnson's smug expression for knowing it. He was favored in the agency and seen as a man who had earned his place as supervisor and confidant to the current generation of Pinkerton brothers. Casey had such lofty aspirations when she was accepted into the agency, and she asked herself, more often of late, how much she had accomplished.

"I would like to speak with any witnesses first."

"There was only one witness who has already been deemed of no value."

Casey pushed her chair back and stood. "Everything in a case has value. Has it been so long since you have been in the field that you have forgotten something so fundamental?"

Johnson also stood, though with delay and a measure of disdain. Casey knew she had pushed her response too far when he lost his false smile. "It is because of your uncle that I do not have you reprimanded. The witness is of no value because they only thought they saw something happen. It was too dark and their recollection of the events changed three times."

Casey dismissed the idea immediately. There was *always* someone, somewhere, who sees something. "Who requested my presence on this case?"

"You mean, who *ordered* you on this case?"

She nodded once to avoid saying aloud the retort on her tongue. Yes, it was definitely the orders getting to her.

"Orders are what they are. You were requested by Mr. Huckabee."

"The man whose money was stolen?" Casey considered it good luck or perhaps bad luck. She would have to reserve judgment. If the client had requested her, then Johnson's posturing threats could be ignored. Her sister had warned her more than once before that it was better to play by the rules than suffer the consequences. Of course, Rose lived her life independent of an agency and made her own rules. Curious why she was requested, and who the client knew well enough for her to receive the assignment, remained at the forefront of her thoughts. She did not, however, share them aloud.

"It is Mr. Huckabee's brother who was killed."

Casey knew Johnson left something out of his briefing, but trying to ferret it out of him would be a waste of her time. She preferred to trust firsthand research over secondhand accounts. "I will leave for Durango in the morning. Good evening, Mr. Johnson."

"Wait." Johnson walked around the table and held out another envelope. "You will need this when you meet the client."

She stared at the envelope before accepting it. "What is it?"

"The client knows you by reputation only. These will verify your identity."

"So will my badge."

Johnson's smug smile returned. "Not this time. Good night, Miss McKenzie, and do not disappoint us."

Casey stuffed the envelope in her duster pocket without opening it. She glanced around the dining room to find a waiter clearing the table the other diner had occupied. The lights were turned low and the staff no doubt wished to close. No train would come through until morning. She thought once more of the comfortable bathtub waiting at the Denver house and sighed at the thought of the brass hip tub with tepid water she could get sent to her room upstairs.

Casey stepped outside and stood for a few seconds while she surveyed the quiet town. She preferred the small, sleepy towns to the noise and traffic of Denver. Thinking of the city recalled her sister and the letter she owed. A telegram would have to suffice until she could sit down and do a letter justice.

A ruckus started up at a nearby saloon, one of the few establishments in town still open. The noise shifted to laughter and the piano playing continued, indicating it was nothing serious. Casey followed a path down the short street to the sheriff's office, where she knew a single jail in the back of the building held Fletcher Jones.

A few minutes later, she was back in her room and opening the envelope she'd stuffed into her pocket. She plopped down on the edge of the bed and stared at the official orders, though it was the extra note that held her concentration. "Of all the ridiculous . . . no, I'm not doing this." Casey crumbled the paper and tossed it across the room.

She stripped down to her chemise and pantalettes and ignored the ball of paper. She forgot about her bath, slipped into bed, and stared at the ceiling. The eerie quiet of the hotel surprised her, for she knew five other patrons slept beneath the same roof. Even the noise from the saloon sounded farther away than previous nights.

Casey was processing what to do next when an explosion rocked the windows. She rolled off the bed and spent a moment untangling her legs from under the sheet. Screams filled the once-quiet air and drowned out the shouts of men outside. She crawled across the room, careful to remain below the window in case of another explosion.

Casey pulled herself up and hid behind the curtains to watch the activity on the street below. Remnants of a wagon lay strewn about the dirt road, and the front of the building across the way was missing its front door and windows.

QUINN MORGAN RUSHED into the street and shielded his face

from the heat of the fire. He might have been cold without his coat and hat had it not been for the adrenaline pumping through his body. He caught sight of a skirt as a woman rounded the wagon, but she disappeared behind the dwindling flames. Shouts from men and women reached him as he followed the skirt.

"You worthless drunk. You could have burned half the town down with your stunt!"

The skirt in question was in fact part of a nightgown peeking from beneath a canvas duster. Boots, similar to his own, completed an ensemble that left little to the imagination.

"Need some help?"

More striking than he remembered from his glimpse of her at the restaurant, the woman looked in his direction after she yanked on the other man's coat. After two failed attempts, she nodded toward the drunken man. "Were you just talking to hear your voice, or did you mean to help?"

Quinn cleared a few sparks that jumped when someone tossed water on the flames and stepped up to help her. The good-for-nothing reeked of cheap whiskey and slurred his complaint at the rough handling. Quinn heaved the man up and braced him against one of the beams on the store now missing its front windows.

The woman moved closer and smacked the drunk across his face. "You're lucky there weren't people in the wagon or in the store."

"Sthphm meh dronuk."

"I don't speak the language of drunk idiots." She raised a hand and called out to someone else. Quinn watched the sheriff run over, with one hand holding his hat in place and the other on his gun.

"Det—Miss McKenzie. What have you got?"

"An idiot who spent too much time in the saloon tonight. I found him trying to light a cigar, and a lot of spent matches strewn about. One must have ended up in the wagon." She pointed to the wagon, now in pieces. "Any idea what was in there, Sheriff? I saw your deputy panic when I first came out."

To Quinn's surprise, the sheriff's face became an unremarkable shade of red.

"Powder. It wasn't supposed to be here."

Quinn handed the derelict over to the sheriff. "I believe he'll find your jail comfortable enough for tonight."

The sheriff tipped his hat and hauled the man away.

"It's a chilly night."

She nodded.

Quinn grinned. "Some might think it's too cold for anything but long underwear." Miss McKenzie—he'd like to know her given name—pulled and overlapped the edges of her duster. "Might help."

She narrowed her gaze at him. "I've seen you before. The restaurant."

"You saw me, and I saw you."

"Are you following me?"

"You mean, did I contrive to have the foolish deputy leave a wagon with gunpowder across from the hotel, hoping a drunk imbecile would strike too many matches, thus causing one to hit the powder and—"

Quinn swore he heard her growl, but to be safe, he cast a glance around to make sure they were still alone or as alone as two people can be in an open street. The water-soaked wagon and ruined powder stood between them and everyone else. He smoothed his grin into a straight line and held up both hands in defense. "My apologies, Miss McKenzie." He held out one of his hands to her. "Quinn Morgan."

"Miss McKenzie."

His mouth quirked. "An unusual forename. Your parents had an odd sense of humor." This time Quinn was certain the growl came from her.

She tugged her duster as tightly as she could manage, revealing more in the process than she likely intended. With only a heated glance that Quinn decided to mistake in part for attraction, Miss McKenzie tromped back to the hotel. He watched her short journey and smiled when she veered right and headed for the side entrance to avoid the small crowd of people who had gathered out front.

CHAPTER 4

Casey managed a few hours of agitated sleep before the sun peeked through the window, having found an easy path to her face through the two curtains she forgot to close all the way upon her return to the room after the unfortunate encounter with whatever or whoever he was. What an embarrassment.

She always knew the whats, whos, and everything in between, and that, she thought smugly, is why she excelled in her chosen profession. Smugness quickly evaporated to let embarrassment return. Even more unsettling was the man's ability to throw her off steady footing, and what, tease her? She might have appreciated the efforts under different circumstances but not last night.

The reflection in the mirror brought her focus back to her upcoming task. She studied the woman staring back at her, shifted her hat a little to the right, and nodded once. Satisfied with her appearance, and grateful she had shaken out the wrinkles the night before, Casey secured the lid of her trunk, picked up her smaller valise, and left the room.

Outside the hotel, a quiet street welcomed her. Someone had removed the wagon, though the ground still appeared wet in a few spots, and they had boarded up the windows from the exploded shop. She enjoyed the faded blue of early morning and the crisp autumn air that accompanied it. Smoke from chimneys released a woodsy aroma and reminded her of the two weeks she spent sleeping under the stars in pursuit of a ne'er-do-well who thought he could get away with killing his former best friend and running off with the former best friend's wife.

She caught him, of course, but it was the memory of campfire and dark skies bursting with millions of stars that eased into her thoughts now. A man coughed nearby and headed to the well in the center of town, drawing Casey back to the present. She made her way to the Queen Anne style train depot, found a porter, and paid him to return to the hotel for her trunk. He almost declined until she pressed the silver coin into his palm.

"Be right back, miss." He tipped his hat and hurried in the direction from which she'd just come. Casey would much rather be on the afternoon train, heading north toward Denver. Resigned to the task ahead, she sighed and purchased her ticket.

"Wait there!" The ticket agent called out to a young man leading a magnificent chestnut horse. "Sorry, miss. Here's your ticket. Train leaves in ten minutes." The agent hurried out of his minuscule office and rushed to the young man's side. She ignored them in favor of boarding and finding a quiet seat on the train, but Casey paused long enough to admire the sleek lines of the gorgeous animal.

QUINN HAD ALWAYS considered himself a lucky man. Skill and a quick mind certainly contributed to his successes, but he never discounted the modest part luck played in a man's life.

Today, all credit for whatever was about to happen rested in the capable hands of Lady Luck. He spent the precious few hours of sleep he'd managed dreaming of long, thick waves and eyes a shade that fell somewhere between blue and gray, like the early morning sky as a storm begins to stir. His stomach tightened as he watched her watching everyone else.

She had paid premium to ride in the almost-empty car save for a young couple, the woman heavy with child, a man who Quinn deduced was a traveling gambler, and an old woman dressed as if she'd stepped out of a big-city department store.

He did not expect to see *her* again. From his vantage point between the two cars, he avoided her scrutiny, but still, he watched her like a freezing man in want of fire. Only luck explained how they ended up on the same train, and he would never regard Fortune in the same way again.

Quinn rolled the proverbial dice and stepped into her line of sight.

Their gazes met. A smile touched the edges of his mouth as her eyes widened, then narrowed into the same expression she'd bestowed upon him during their stimulating encounter the night before. He'd received more encouragement from women, but not a single invitation—in this case, an invitation to keep away—enticed him more than the one she offered now.

The aisle seemed to shrink as he entered the car and sat on the high-backed bench opposite her. "We meet again."

"You have a knack for stating the obvious."

His smile widened. "So do you, since you mentioning it is also stating the obvious."

"What are you doing here?"

"The same thing you are, I presume—riding the train to get from one place to another."

Her perfectly formed lips pursed. "Find another seat. Better yet, find another train."

"Sorry, but this train is going where I need to go, and I have a schedule to keep." Quinn enjoyed the flush that colored her cheeks to a faint rosy hue. The blush complemented the hair he thought was more the color of his gelding's coat, but in the light of day, he changed his mind, even as his fingers itched to release the auburn locks from pins and hat.

"Then find another seat."

"Have I offended you, Miss McKenzie?" Quinn leaned into the back of the bench. "If you recall, I apologized last night."

"Fine. I accept your apology." She withdrew a book from her valise and held it up to her nose.

Quinn stole the opportunity to peruse her at his leisure. Her ensemble suited her, though one would not find the likes of it in a catalog or store, leading him to think she had it made. She could not walk into any room—or anywhere else—without drawing notice. "An unusual name, 'Miss.' However did your parents choose it?"

Casey snapped the book closed and lowered it to her lap. "Are you always this obnoxious?"

He grinned unrepentantly. "Considering how we met, and your attire at the time, asking your Christian name does not seem an obnoxious question."

This time, her blush heightened the color from her neck on up. Quinn decided blush was a becoming color on Miss McKenzie.

"Will you leave me alone if I tell you?"

Quinn shrugged, gaining the expected low growl. He rather admired how she managed such a sound without lessening her femininity.

"Cassandra."

He studied her quietly for a few seconds before shaking his head. "Somehow, you do not look like a 'Cassandra.'"

"And what, pray tell, do I look like?"

Quinn shrugged. "I will let you know when I find out."

"This is a ridiculous conversation. Now, go away." She opened her book again and ignored him.

Quinn chuckled and made himself as comfortable on the bench as possible. He was used to going without sleep and doubted he would get much rest now, sitting across from her. No, he thought to himself, she does not look like a Cassandra, but as his mind relaxed, her name and face replaced all other thoughts.

CASEY PEERED OVER the top of her book every fifteen minutes to gauge if he was really sleeping. His chest rose and fell with even breaths, but she could not see much of his face, covered as it was by his black hat. She remembered his hazel eyes leaned toward a green that reminded her of tall summer grass under a bright sun. His dark hair brushed his collar and matched his neatly trimmed beard. He was a little too tall, a little too broad, and a little too *everything*.

She couldn't focus on the novel and slipped the book into her valise. Casey caught sight of the few sheets of paper and pencil she'd brought along and thought again of the letter she owed her sister.

With a touch of resignation, she removed the paper and pencil, and the book to hold the paper flat. She pressed the tip of the pencil to paper and weighed her words. She was more used to sending off a few words in a telegram than writing a letter.

Dear Rose,

The last assignment proved less uneventful than I originally expected. I am glad it's over,

> *for the quarry proved a tiresome chase in the last week. As I mentioned in my telegram, the sheriff made an arrest, and Colorado Springs is now safer for it. Unfortunately, I must delay the visit home I mentioned in my last telegram. I am on my way to Durango for a new assignment that came up unexpectedly. Please offer my apologies to Mrs. Pennyworth. She probably already had the room prepared just the way I like it.*

A smile touched Casey's lips as she thought of the loving housekeeper, who didn't have a problem raising a brow at any behavior she deemed unladylike. Then, of course, Mrs. Pennyworth could also shoot a gun with surprising skill. Casey always thought the housekeeper secretly enjoyed the girls' spirited misadventures.

Casey's thoughts drifted without prompting to Quinn as he pretended to slumber in the seat across from her. Of course, she assumed he put on the act for her benefit, or perhaps he simply wanted to discourage conversation. Casey ignored her wayward speculations and returned to the letter.

> *Have you heard of the Huckabee Mining Company? It is Mr. Huckabee I am to meet. The circumstances are rather unfortunate, but it is my hope the situation will be resolved quickly. I appreciate the opportunity to visit*

> *Durango since it has been ages, though I was rather looking forward to spending a little time at home.*

Yes, Casey thought, Rose would appreciate a bit of sentiment.

> *Have you blown up anything in the house again? I do envy you sometimes; your independence from anyone else's command (do not tell Mrs. Pennyworth I said so, or she will be scandalized to think she is not our major general).*

She sneaked another glance at Quinn and found him to be in the same position, with his black hat covering the top half of his face. How, she wondered, did he remain so still?? This was the worst part of travel for her—the sitting.

> *Forgive me, sister, for the brief letter. I promise to make it up the next time. By the way, any good cases lately?*
> *Love,*
> *Casey*

Casey watched the landscape pass and spent the time between reading and trying to figure out what Quinn Morgan might be thinking. By the time the train pulled into the first rest depot on her trek west, she realized the time had escaped her notice. Her unwanted traveling companion did not move when the train rolled to stop, and she took advantage of his inactivity to put away her things, hug her valise close to her chest, and ease away as quietly as possible.

She missed his slow smile and lazy stretch as he watched her depart the train car.

CHAPTER 5

The bustling mining town of Durango, with a population of a few thousand souls and nestled in a spacious river valley with the rugged La Plata Mountains of the San Juan range as a majestic backdrop, hummed with activity. Snow capped the distant peaks and dusted the sides of the mountains, making way for the yellow-and-gold aspens to take center stage in one of nature's stunning displays.

The spent blossoms of the rabbitbrush shrub mixed with sagebrush to dot the landscape among pines and ponderosas. A variety of vegetation—none of which Casey could call by name—covered untouched sections of hillsides. She suspected Rose would know the scientific names for each of the trees and shrubs.

Smoke from the smelter and soot from the train marred an otherwise clear, afternoon sky. Casey had spent so much time on trains during her time with the Pinkertons and not given much thought to what they and the mines did to the landscape. Progress, she mused, was not worth some sacrifices. She smiled thinking of her sister, who enjoyed modern conveniences and contraptions that allowed her to conduct her experiments. She would not be surprised if Rose invented something truly remarkable one day.

Casey did not have a head for science or contraptions. Her gun and the two legs God gave her were all she needed—most days. There was always hot, running water and oversized bathtubs to consider.

She handed her ticket to the porter so he could retrieve her trunk, after giving him instructions on delivery.

"You'll be wanting a ride to the hotel, miss."

"I'm content to walk, but thank you," she informed the porter.

He looked her over and said again, "I reckon that's not a good idea, miss. One of the hired carriages will take you for a dime."

Casey decided not to reprimand the young man for thinking she was incapable of taking care of herself. True, wearing her current attire of action-hindering skirts, she carried only a small pistol in her reticule, and another in a hidden holster.

"A walk is just the thing after the journey. My destination is not far." She found two dimes in her bag and handed them to the porter. "Please see the trunk is delivered."

She left the young man staring after her, grateful now she chose not to travel in her preferred riding skirt, simple blouse, and duster. She selected each outfit for a specific purpose, and this one served to hide her true intention but not so much that she received too much scrutiny.

The two-block distance to The Strater Hotel afforded her a chance to stretch her legs after an interminably long train ride. Her erstwhile traveling companion had vanished from the first-class car after the initial rest-station stop, and she completed the trip in solitude and boredom. Not even the antics of Sherlock Holmes and Dr. Watson in *A Study in Scarlet* could keep her mind from straying every so often to Quinn Morgan before drifting to the upcoming case.

As she passed a grocery and saloon, and farther down a bookstore, which she made a note to visit before leaving, and various other establishments, she tried to reason why, if Mr. Huckabee was murdered, did the police simply give up. According to what little information Johnson provided, one Mr. Frank Huckabee died in his office late on a Tuesday night, hours after the rest of his staff went home. His brother, Ellison, whom Casey was to meet within the hour, said his brother never worked past five o'clock since he was an early riser.

She ignored the glances of men and kept as far from the dust in the roads as possible while she sorted out how to approach Ellison Huckabee. Casey noted the stockyard across the way before she entered The Strater Hotel, where unknown man who did not appear to work there immediately greeted her.

"Miss McKenzie?"

"Yes."

"The porter at the rail station hired me to deliver your trunk."

"Thank you. Sorry, your name?"

He rushed to remove his hat. "Jeb Crinks, ma'am."

"Thank you, Mr. Crinks. The hotel . . ." Casey left the man bemused with her unfinished sentence, but she had little choice when her mind and mouth refused to work together. No scenario she might have imagined explained Quinn Morgan's presence at the front desk in the lobby.

WHERE CASSANDRA MCKENZIE was concerned, Quinn's curiosity had remained unconstrained since their first encounter. He sensed the moment she realized his presence, but he did not wait in the lobby to find out if she planned to confront him or ignore him. The uncertainty added another layer of interesting questions to a growing list about the woman.

He accepted the key from the man behind the counter with a guarantee that his luggage would be up right away. Quinn proceeded up the main staircase to the second floor and down the quiet hallway.

"Mr. Morgan, what are you doing here?"

Quinn erased his smile before he pivoted. "To sleep, as I imagine everyone does when staying in a hotel."

She clamped a hand on his arm as he reached to slide the key into the door. "Again, what are *you* doing *here*?"

The door opened with a quick turn of the knob and Quinn held it open for her.

"Absolutely not."

"I have no intention of arguing in the hall, so if you would like to continue this conversation, then you will have to join me inside." Quinn thought perhaps he'd pushed too far when she opened her reticule and reached inside. "I don't think so." He pulled her into the room and immediately let go once she was inside but kept her bag. Quinn reached in and pulled out the revolver. "Surprising choice. Of course, a derringer that fit neatly in your pocket would suit you less than your name."

He palmed the Remington revolver to test its weight, though he knew well enough what it could do in the hands of someone skilled enough to wield it. Quinn dropped it back in the bag and passed it over. "Does everyone call you Cassandra?"

"What is your obsession with my name anyway?" Casey tied the strings and held the bag close. "You dragged me in here, Mr. Morgan. Perhaps now you'll tell me what you're doing in Durango and this hotel? There are plenty of other accommodations in town."

Quinn removed his hat and tossed it on the bed. "Even more surprising than that pistol you carry, Miss McKenzie, is your utter lack of fear. Who are you?"

"Perhaps I'm good at masking fear, and you still haven't answered *my* question."

He crossed the room to leave the path open between her and

the door. She did not leave. Quinn glanced out one of the four windows to glimpse views of both town and mountains. Miners, townsfolk, and tourists bustled about on the roads below, each one easy to pick out from the next. "I have business in Durango, and an acquaintance recommended the hotel. Your turn. What are *you* doing here?"

"A question for a question, and you have already asked yours. Who am I? Cassandra McKenzie. How odd you should forget so soon." Casey started for the open door, but a few steps away from freedom, she turned around. "It behooves me to warn you that if you are following me, the chase will not end well—for you."

Amusement fled as he approached her. "You are either too arrogant to not care who you might be up against, or you are proficient enough with that weapon to negate the need for caution. I wonder, Miss McKenzie, which it will turn out to be."

A raised brow and half-smile were all the answers she provided before leaving the room. Quinn closed the door and braced himself long enough to bring both his anger and attraction under control. He came to Durango for a job, and though he had yet to accept or turn it down, he may have found another reason to remain in town.

CHAPTER 6

Casey studied the brick building situated between an impressive Romanesque-style bank and the bookstore she had passed earlier on her way to the hotel. Housed within the wide, brick structure was Huckabee Mining Company's offices, where Ellison Huckabee no doubt waited and wondered at her delay. She silently cursed Quinn Morgan, but she would not be rushed.

She lingered in one place long enough for a few passersby to move down the road and leave her with an unobstructed view of the surrounding businesses, including another bank, hotel, bookstore, and to her delight, a bakery. Johnson's report did not specify which bank was robbed, and neither she couldn't see from a distance which ones appeared vulnerable. Durango's turbulent history of gunfights in the street and general lawlessness was a thing of the past, at least by outward appearances.

Casey knew how quickly circumstances could change on the streets of a booming mining town. Even prosperous men and women were not immune. She had read how the Huckabees made an impressive fortune first off copper from Utah's canyons, then moved to Colorado where they amassed more wealth from gold and silver. Their evident success and prominence were no doubt why they believed themselves worth a Pinkerton agent's time.

Turning back to study Huckabee's building, she noted the iron bars on the inside of the windows. One wouldn't notice them at first glance, but upon closer inspection, a talented architect designed the bars in a way to make a patron of the building feel secure, rather than caged in.

"Clever, Mr. Huckabee," Casey murmured. The mining company's name was etched across the clean windows, so clean she could see all the goings-on behind her. If she hadn't been on Main Avenue in daylight, she would have used the pistol Quinn admired earlier to erase the grin off his face.

She whirled around, though no one else stood close enough to hear them. Casey poked him in the chest with a gloved finger. "You're not keen on keeping your feet, are you? Because I'm thinking that's where the first two bullets are going to land."

"A woman has yet to be hanged in Colorado, but for my sake, I hope the marshal finds a good hanging tree for you if you make good on your threat."

"All I would need in my defense are a few people who have met you, then I'd be set free."

Quinn did not smile this time, but a light of amusement

flickered in his eyes and caused Casey to step back. "Excuse me, Mr. Morgan. I have somewhere to be." She stepped to the door and still felt his closeness. He wasn't going anywhere. "The fates cannot hate me this much."

He eased around her and opened the door himself. "It would seem, Miss McKenzie, the fates know exactly what they are doing."

Casey muttered a curse she was certain her sister and mother would cringe to hear, and Quinn's chuckle only fanned the proverbial flames of her annoyance. Without a backward glance or another word, she brushed past him and entered the offices of Huckabee Mining Company. Casey ignored Quinn in favor of the slight and tidy man standing behind a long counter and offered her name.

"Miss McKenzie to see Mr. Huckabee. He is expecting me."

The man assessed her quickly, and his expression did not change when he gave the same brief appraisal to Quinn, who now held his fine black hat in one hand. "Mr. Morgan, I presume?"

"You presume correctly."

The assistant—Casey assumed that is what he was—nodded once. "I am Linwood. Mr. Huckabee is expecting you."

Casey interrupted Linwood's walk toward the hall entrance. "Excuse me? Expecting which of us?"

Linwood peered at her through a pair of round, wire-rimmed spectacles. "Both of you, of course."

"Of course."

Quinn leaned close to her as they followed Linwood down a hallway and past offices devoid of activity or people. "This should be interesting."

She slowed her pace and ground out through barely opened lips, "Do you have a death wish?"

"I have never met a woman so quick to temper."

"I promise, you will regret—"

"Ah, too late."

Casey was saved from making an utter fool of herself when Linwood stopped in front of a studded wood door with brass hardware and an ornate pane of glass cut into the top center. On either side of the door, two long windows gave the occupant a full view of anyone coming or going.

Linwood stood in front of the glass for a few seconds before the man on the other side waved him in. The assistant opened the door and stepped aside so Casey and Quinn could enter. Mr. Huckabee, a robust man of greater-than-average height with graying hair and a perfectly trimmed mustache, motioned them into his office. He waited until Linwood closed the door before he offered either of them a seat.

"Miss McKenzie." Huckabee looked her over. "You are not entirely what I expected."

Used to subtle misconceptions about her appearance, Casey brushed past his comment with one of her own. "It would seem you are covering all contingencies with me *and* Mr. Morgan."

Huckabee's gray brows raised, and his lips thinned into a line. "Do you have a problem, Mr. Morgan, working with Miss McKenzie?"

"I work alone."

Casey did not look at Quinn, though all his teasing and charm from before had vanished when he spoke those three simple words. Curiosity about Quinn Morgan rose a few more notches.

"I see." Huckabee tapped the top of his desk before sitting in the leather chair behind it. "And do you, Miss McKenzie, work alone?"

"It prevents differences of opinion."

"Agent Johnson assured me there would be no problem."

"I did not say I wouldn't work the case, Mr. Huckabee." Casey refused to admit she had little choice in the matter if she wanted to keep her badge. Johnson had obviously briefed him on the necessity to keep who and what she was confidential. "I was told to provide you with proof of my identity, yet you seem unconcerned."

"Your supervisor described you well enough, Miss McKenzie. If you prefer the formality, then I will accept the document."

Casey removed the official order from her reticule and handed it to Huckabee, who simply dropped it on the desk without unfolding the paper. She hadn't needed the document, so why had Johnson insisted she bring it? "Where does Mr. Morgan come in?"

"Mr. Morgan can speak for himself."

Quinn sat back in the chair, affecting a somewhat lazy demeanor, yet his taut muscles did not move beneath the finely cut suit he wore. "And I have not decided if I will come in at all."

Huckabee rose from his chair, perhaps thinking his imposing height would get his point across better, and said, "I have made a more than fair offer of compensation for your services, Mr. Morgan."

Quinn, who stood two inches above six feet, did not find Huckabee's posturing impressive. "It is my offer to accept or deny, and while I am inclined to accept, I won't work with anyone who keeps secrets." He looked sharply at Casey.

Casey stood, surprising both men. Quinn quickly followed suit, and Huckabee leaned back, putting a little more distance between them. "Mr. Huckabee, I agreed to work on this case because of your brother's death. I will do my best to find the stolen money, but you must understand that is secondary."

Huckabee considered her terms for several seconds before agreeing. "My staff will be at your disposal for questions. Linwood will provide you with all the information you will need."

Casey thanked him and left the office. Once she was at Linwood's station, she realized Quinn had not followed her this time.

STARS SPECKLED THE clear night sky by the time Quinn left one of the town's finer dining establishments. He replayed the unusual exchange between Miss McKenzie and Mr. Huckabee over and over in his mind, and while he had Huckabee figured out, the brazen Cassandra was a puzzle, and he looked forward to figuring out where each piece fit.

His private discussion with Huckabee following her departure had done more to sour him toward helping the man, and yet, he sensed Cassandra's conviction in following through with her job. The more he said her name in his thoughts, the more he saw how it could suit her.

Quinn entered the hotel and acknowledged the desk clerk before ascending the stairs and walking down the hall to his room. The key turned easily, and once inside, he leaned his back against the door and smiled. He spoke to the dark figure in the room without looking her way. "I imagine the hotel will not look kindly upon the violation of a guest's privacy."

A match struck and a small flame flickered to life. In a matter of seconds, the lone lamp on a table by the window came to life and illuminated the woman sitting casually in the chair.

"Ah, there you are." Quinn walked to the center of the room but did not sit down, for Cassandra occupied the only chair. He had not bothered to turn on the electric light, enjoying the way she looked in the softer glow. It would serve her right if he made himself comfortable on the bed. "I'm certain I locked the door upon my arrival."

"You did."

Quinn discarded his hat on the bed and removed his long, black duster but made no move to remove any other clothing. "Once I gave myself a little time, your name triggered a memory of a visit I made last year to Denver. There was mention of a woman by the name of Rose McKenzie, a detective of sorts. There was, however, no mention of a relative in a similar profession, which is curious."

"You clearly have nothing better to do with your time than wonder about me, which I find curious."

"Oh, my curiosity regarding you is quite a good use of my time, Miss McKenzie, or shall I dispense with pretenses and call you Agent McKenzie?"

CASEY TAPPED HER fingers on the table's empty wooden surface and studied him. She set aside all annoyances regarding his unwanted presence in her life and preoccupations with his charm and dissected what she saw before her.

She quickly dismissed him as a lawman. Everything about his behavior spoke of man answerable only to himself—like Rose. The tiny twinge of envy resurfaced before she quickly squashed it. "No one calls me 'Agent' anything."

"Yes, Huckabee mentioned as much." Quinn tapped the side of his head. "I have an excellent memory. Your sister—interesting story, and not one I'm sure I believe."

"It's probably true," Casey mumbled as she thought of the last time Rose blew something up on accident.

"Fascinating." Quinn crossed the room and removed a few small objects from his jacket pocket to set on the dresser. "Now, let us move past this little dance—"

"I don't dance and certainly wouldn't with you." Casey slid her fingers over the table as she left the chair. "But yes, let us move past it. Which is it, lawyer or bounty hunter, though neither will get me to agree to work with you?"

"You hold both lawyers and bounty hunters in poor esteem."

"One isn't much better than the other." Casey brushed by him but stopped before opening the door. "Decline the job."

"Can't do that."

"Why ever not?"

Quinn moved slowly toward her.

No, Casey thought, he stalked like a man closing in on prey.

"Because, I am unexpectedly, and much to my surprise, looking forward to the wedding."

CHAPTER 7

Casey considered herself in control of her emotions, at least all of them except anger, which in her defense she only directed at those who deserved it. In the company of family, she often shared hilarity and plenty of eye rolling but only because she was with people she did not need to impress. Therefore, the abrupt giggle that escaped her lips caught her by surprise.

She attempted to stifle the laughter, then gave up. Casey put an extra foot of space between them and allowed her amusement to dwindle before she met Quinn's gaze. "I can see you are serious or at least hoped I was serious, but truly, you can't have expected me to swoon from shock or shout in indignation."

Quinn tossed up his hands in a gesture of defeat and reassessed his options before he sat on the edge of the bed. She did not have any problem entering a man's room in the middle of the night and would not be constrained by formalities. "Any normal woman would have done one of those."

Casey sobered a little. Pleased with the unforeseen

entertainment, she moved farther into the room again to stand a few feet in front of Quinn. "You are both."

He glanced up at her. "Pardon?"

"Lawyer and bounty hunter, though how one becomes the other I could not guess. It must be quite a story."

"I assure you it is not." He once again wore the expression of a predator who had his target right where he wanted it. "You can't decline the job, and even if you could, you already told Huckabee you wouldn't."

Casey held up three fingers. "Point of fact, I can decline it." She lowered the first finger. "I choose not to turn it down because I despise people who think they can get away with breaking the law and killing people." She tucked the second finger away. "And I work alone." She dropped her arm to her side.

Quinn pushed off the bed. "I'm not turning the job down, either, and yes, I was serious about the wedding."

The rumpled quilt immediately drew Casey's notice. When she looked at him again, she wanted to swipe at his grin. "No, you weren't."

He shrugged. "Not in the literal sense, but when I laid out the plan to Huckabee, he agreed it was plausible enough not to draw suspicion in the town and will allow us to be seen together whenever necessary."

"I am not sharing a room with you."

"Such distrust. Of course, I do not intend for us to share a room."

Casey waved aside his idea and started for the door. "I will take care of Huckabee, and after this moment, we won't have to see each other again." Casey gripped the handle. "You locked it?"

Quinn smiled. "You entered without a key. Exiting should be no more difficult."

She held out a gloved hand and waited for him to bring her the key, which he surprised her by doing. Casey unlocked the door and left the key in the lock when she opened it. "Why is this so important to you?"

"The case or working with you?"

"Either. Both. We can start with the case."

All traces of humor left his face and revealed an almost savage guise to his hazel eyes. This was not a man to be toyed with, Casey thought, and while nothing he did now caused her alarm, she did not doubt this man was an effective lawyer—and bounty hunter.

Quinn closed no more distance between them, and he did not need to for his energy to warm the skin safely beneath her clothes. "Does it matter why when I am not leaving?"

"I think it matters to you." Casey scrutinized his face closely and caught the faint and brief twitch at the corner of one eye. "If you want to work with me, then I have to be able to trust you."

"You have already made it clear you don't work with anyone—ever."

"And our acquaintance ends here and now if you do not answer me."

His smirk implied he found her words amusing. "I believe you mean it, and if given the choice, I believe Huckabee would choose you and your Pinkerton badge over me and my lack of one." Quinn held up his arms as though sweeping empty air and walked farther into the room. "You already do trust me, or at least as much as I imagine you allow yourself to trust, but you'll get no answer from me save this: If we do not maintain justice, justice will not maintain us."

"Francis Bacon," Casey murmured, though Quinn's quick raise of his brow indicated he had heard her.

"You know your philosophers?"

Casey shook her head. "No. You will hear from me one way or the other." She exited the room and closed the door behind her. Casey did not want the confines of her room just then. Darkness had long since settled on the town, which meant venturing outdoors was not an option, at least not in her current attire.

She found the way to her room, half in a daze and with the other half of her brain trying to figure out Quinn's motive for taking this case. Once inside, with the door locked, Casey opened the window to let in fresh air, and with it came faint sounds from the saloon district. It took her record time to remove the outfit she'd worn since departing the train. Her trunk contained only one suitable evening dress, but Casey tended to avoid situations where she might require an extra change of clothing for the sole purpose of doing what was proper. Unless, of course, she was in Denver with her sister or visiting her mother, and then she behaved as a well-bred woman should.

"What is he up to?" Which one, Casey silently added. She tossed the long-sleeved flared jacket on the bed and soon added the belt, shirtwaist, and skirt to the pile, leaving her in a camisole, petticoat, and her version of a more pliable, custom-made corset.

"Huckabee wants to find his brother's killer, but he also wants his money back. Which one does he want more?" Casey sat on a padded bench at the end of the bed to remove a silver-bladed dagger from the sheath in her brown, heeled boots. The long laces gave her some trouble, but she could not take a knife to them as she had the last corset. To get a new pair of stylish boots made for her purposes would require a trip to her sister's magician of a shoemaker in Denver. After taking a few deep breaths, Casey managed the laces, slipped the boots off, and wiggled her toes.

Casey continued the conversation with herself as she paced the room. "Why does Huckabee need a Pinkerton *and* a bounty hunter? What does he know that he doesn't want us to learn?"

Finally somewhat loose-limbed and comfortable, she sat at the desk and stared at the journey entry she started earlier, after the meeting with Huckabee and Quinn.

Durango is as expected, bustling and noisy sometimes, quiet at other times. Far too much dust and smoke, but ruggedly beautiful beneath, like a woman of great beauty trying to dim her appeal as not to attract unwanted attention.

Casey smiled at the last description and blamed analogy on reading too many novels. She gently bit the corner of her lower lip as a face intruded, and she continued.

There is an unexpected setback by the name of Quinn Morgan. He showed up at Ellison Huckabee's mining office, after our encounter on the train out of Colorado Springs. Why is he here? He doesn't appear to need the work or . . .

Her thoughts had muddled after writing those few sentences, and even now, a task that usually brought clarity annoyed her. She closed the journal and returned it to her satchel before staring at the open window. The cool night air beckoned her closer. Casey knelt in front of the window, rested her chin on the ledge, and stared up at the brilliant splash of stars across a sky bathed in shades of blue from dark to darker.

The berating began as her mind cleared. Nothing excused her lack of professionalism in leaving the meeting early. Quinn . . . no, she had to stop blaming him. Curiosity, more than anything else kept her from packing her bags, turning in her badge, and walking away.

"Well, now you've gone and done it, Casey," she said to the sky. Frustrated and hungry, she cast a longing glance at the bed before standing and walking over to her trunk. From within, she pulled out more comfortable clothes than she had worn earlier and dressed. A glance at the clock had her smiling. "It will serve him right."

CHAPTER 8

The smoky saloon offered enough wretchedness to take Quinn's mind off the woman occupying a room a few doors down from him at the hotel. He had waited and listened until he heard her door open and close, and when enough time had passed, he locked his room and found the best of the lower-end saloons in town rather than visit the bar at the hotel.

The corner table, tucked far enough away from everyone else, afforded Quinn a view of the entire room, including the entrance and stairs that curved to a second level. No doubt patrons occupied the rooms above while the barkeep kept whiskey flowing and glasses filled.

A bald man in a striped shirt played a lively rendition of "Climbing over the Rocky Mountain," or at least his version of it. Quinn doubted Gilbert and Sullivan would approve, but some patrons tapped their feet while others danced with comely serving girls. What did he know?

He'd seen the inside of as many saloons as he had courthouses and law offices, and in his mind, the clientele changed little from one to the next. Businessmen in fine suits drank next to miners with soot-stained fingers, and as long as they could enjoy their libations in peace, Quinn suspected they cared little who sat next to them. Come tomorrow, in the honest light of day, they would feel differently. The women pouring drinks and seducing men were surprisingly clean with a just-washed look about them.

"Something stronger, mister?"

He glanced down at the thick-walled bottle in his hand, still more than half-full of soda water. "This'll do me." Quinn slid fifty cents across the table to the serving girl.

She eyed the money, and Quinn did not miss the surreptitious glance over her shoulder at a well-dressed woman, her face masked by shadow, in the opposite corner. "Sure I can't get you anything else, mister?"

"Conversation, when your shift is over." Quinn didn't care if she misunderstood his intentions, and from the suggestive way she inched closer, she had. "Who are the regulars in here?" he asked.

She leaned back, this time studying him more closely. "Why'd you want to know?"

"Could be they'll get up a card game soon. I noticed there aren't any going."

The girl shrugged and dropped the fifty cents down the front of her blouse. "You'll want to try the place next door."

"I've never known a saloon where a man can't get up a

friendly game of cards."

This time she sidled a foot closer and whispered, "Not tonight, mister, but if you're looking for a friendly game—"

Glass shattered, and the saloon grew quiet. Quinn ignored the girl and watched a small man holding the neck end of a bottle in one hand and a pistol in the other. The behemoth standing next to him wiped his face. Dropping the bottle, the smaller man withdrew a second pistol and slowly backed out of the saloon. No one tried to stop him. A collective sigh swept through the saloon when the behemoth returned to his drinking.

Quinn kept his seat and continued to watch as the face attached to the smaller form came into view. Beneath the dirt carelessly smeared over smooth skin, familiar eyes remained vigilant as they scanned the room. "Damn her." The noise slowly returned to its former din, but Quinn was more interested in the older woman in the corner who spoke briefly with two men before they also left the saloon. The matron's eyes drifted toward him, as if she sensed him watching her. Quinn asked the serving girl her name.

"Belle."

"Pretty name." Quinn stood, pressed a silver dollar into Belle's hand and casually kissed her cheek. "Take care of yourself, Belle." Without another word to her, Quinn walked slowly from the saloon and once outside, caught sight of the two men rounding a building at the end of the block. He slipped down the narrow alley next to the saloon and ran as fast as he could, coming out on the next block and running into the slim form he sought.

Quinn yanked her back into the alley and covered her mouth with a strong hand. "It's me."

Oddly, those two simple words calmed her immediately. He knew she couldn't see his features clearly in the darkness. "I'm going to let go. Keep quiet until they leave."

Before he could move his hand, she bit down. Once free, she hissed out, "What *are* you doing?"

"Saving you." Quinn shook his hand and rubbed a finger over where he felt her teeth marks. It was not how he imagined her . . . Quinn shook the errant thought away when he heard the rustle of moving bodies. "Quiet."

They waited in the shadows with Quinn's black duster and hat offering them cover. For several seconds, her breath tickled the skin beneath his chin, but she remained still and silent until the men passed.

Quinn's back met the brick wall behind them when she shoved him away.

"That is for your high-handed tactics. I had the situation under control."

He grabbed her arm and dragged her farther down the alley until they stood halfway between each exit. "Those men were going to kill you!" he yelled within a whisper.

"That was the idea, you imbecile!"

CASEY PULLED HER arm free of his grasp and suppressed the urge to rub where his fingers had pressed into her flesh. She considered them even since she had bitten him. "Did you ever actually collect a bounty on anyone or win a legal case?"

"This isn't about me. You're dressed like a man, you were alone in a saloon that, from what I could tell, was operating a business beyond liquor and whores, and you want to question my experience."

"I know all that!" Casey almost swiped the itchy wool cap off her head until she remembered how long it took to pin her thick hair beneath it. "Did it occur to you that I wasn't in there for the atmosphere, that I might actually know what I'm doing?"

"Did it occur to you that whatever lark—"

"Lark? How dare you—"

"Oh, I will dare a lot more." Quinn breathed in deep and back out again. "You didn't see those men's faces when they followed you, Cassandra."

"Casey."

"What?"

She enjoyed throwing him off his rant. "Call me Casey. Only my mother calls me Cassandra, and sometimes Mrs. Pennyworth."

"Mrs. Penny who?"

"Pennyworth. She runs my sister's house in Denver."

"You don't mind when she calls you Cassandra?"

Casey's right brow raised slightly. "No one contradicts Mrs. Pennyworth."

"She sounds formidable."

Casey smiled. "I adore her, and she's quite delightful, except for the time I asked her to call me 'Casey.'"

He perused her from scuffed boots to dirt-smudged face. "Casey suits you, but so does breathing, and they intended to kill you. Why?"

"Well, I would have found out if you had left me to it." Casey pushed him against the brick wall again. "You are not my partner and thank heaven, not my husband—real or otherwise—so leave me alone."

Casey made it back to the small shed where she had stuffed a change of clothing and within fifteen minutes was dressed properly enough to be overlooked when she sneaked into the back entrance of the hotel and up to her room.

A match flared and brought light to the dark room, creating a scene too similar to the one she set up in his room to be a coincidence. A fire burned in the woodstove and warmed the space, indicating he had been in there longer than she might have hoped. Casey turned on the lights to illuminate the room, and a quick study revealed nothing out of place. "How did you get here first?"

"The time it took you to change into your fetching ensemble was all I needed." He sat back in her single chair at the desk. "That same amount of time is all it took for me to realize I owe you an apology."

Casey loved her job, or so she told herself a few times in her head as she dreamed of a quiet room, an enormous bathtub, and a few hours of deep sleep. She did not think housekeeping would appreciate her ringing for hot water this time of night. "It could not have waited until morning?"

"We need to be on speaking terms tomorrow, so no, it had to be tonight." He withdrew a silver pocket watch and studied the face. "Or this morning. Never mind. No, it couldn't wait."

"A gentleman would have seen his error in entering a lady's room, so your gesture—"

"Is justified."

Casey could not argue with the logic, and she was now too tired to do so. "You have apologized, I thank you, and now you must leave." When Quinn stood, Casey noticed for the first time since she entered the room that he still wore his long, black coat. His hat, however, was in his hands.

"Why were you willing to risk your life tonight?"

His question, spoken low and with great sincerity, surprised Casey enough to answer. "I did not risk my life, at least not any more than usual. I did not earn my badge by sitting behind a desk."

"You claimed to always work alone."

"I do."

"Even Kate Warne did not think herself so high above the rest of her fellow agents that she could not work with others." Quinn moved closer to her and made a circular motion around his face. "You missed some."

Casey gritted her teeth and walked past him to the porcelain washbasin. She dipped a clean cloth in the water and rubbed at her skin to remove whatever dirt she had missed in her hasty change in the shed. "Kate Warne had Allan Pinkerton." She waved her hand in front of him. "I have you." She scolded herself when he grinned. "I misspoke, but with your education, you should have been able to grasp my meaning."

"Indeed." Quinn leaned comfortably against the wall near the door.

"Fine." Casey slapped the now-dirty cloth on the washstand. "What did you and Mr. Huckabee discuss after my . . . departure?" She omitted the word "hasty," and Quinn was kind enough not to speak it, either.

"I presented him with an idea, he agreed to a course of action, and I came to find you."

"Lovely. Now, why don't you fill in all the canyon-sized holes in your explanation?"

Quinn did not smile as she expected him to. "Why don't you explain what you were doing in a saloon dressed as a man?"

CHAPTER 9

Casey recalled a case that had put her in the unfortunate situation of facing down a prized bull, which only happened because someone had stolen the bull in question from an extremely influential friend of Colorado's governor. The bull presumably had not enjoyed his first relocation, and he certainly did not wish to go through it again. In the end, the legitimate owner's cowhands wrestled the bull back home, but the incident saw Casey face down in the mud during her attempt to escape the noble beast who liberated himself from the cowhands' clutches.

Quinn's hard expression put her in mind of the bull. It had been too dark in the alley to see his face, and she had been too wound up to pay heed to his rigid stance. Now with her eyes adjusting to the light in the room, she noticed everything from his unyielding posture to the stern set of his mouth and narrowed eyes.

"As I explained before, I was doing my job."

"Dressed like a man? Why not a serving girl or better yet, a whore?"

She flushed under his harsh words, and he must have noticed because he immediately apologized.

"Pardon me. I shouldn't have said that."

"You don't need—" The look he gave her said he did, and she let it go. "Men talk freely when drink loosens their lips. As a girl—or whore—they would have been more interested in me."

His body relaxed somewhat. "I can't figure you out, Casey." He created messy furrows in his hair when he ran his hand through once and then over his face. "Why did they chase after you?"

"Wish I knew. After a few minutes, I noticed one of the two miners next to me glancing at my drink. I hadn't taken a sip, and he must have wondered about it because he kept looking from me to the glass."

"You broke a bottle of whiskey over one of their heads."

"Which is why I got out of there and possibly why they followed." Casey sat on the seat he had vacated earlier. "They were talking about a recent robbery, but I wasn't there long enough to get any details."

"Or they figured out you were a woman."

Casey shook her head. "No one figures out my disguises." She peered up at him. "Except you. How did you know?"

Quinn shrugged. "Lucky guess."

She didn't believe him, but Casey wasn't interested in turning the conversation in another direction. "I have had time to consider all options regarding this case."

"And?" Quinn moved to stand a few feet away from where she sat.

"Huckabee's offices were empty, except for his secretary, Mr. Linwood. Did he mention it?"

"No, and neither did I."

Casey scooted to the edge of the seat. "Because you weren't curious or because . . ."

"I expect you already know the answer." Quinn's gaze drifted momentarily to the clock on the wall.

"Huckabee suspects someone in his employ."

Quinn nodded in agreement.

"This idea of yours has merit."

"Marriage?"

Casey's lips involuntarily pursed, and she gave him her best eye roll. "A pretense only, and there will be rules."

Quinn rested his right forearm on the dresser and an almost-smile appeared on his lips. "There should always be rules."

"You're amused now, which I find disconcerting. Your moods flip and flop from one extreme to the next, which brings me to rule one." Casey stood and held up a single finger. "I have enough to accomplish without trying to figure out what you're thinking, and I have an arrogant supervisor who will need an accounting. If you want to share a thought or idea, do so."

"Does that apply to you as well?"

Casey considered his question a few seconds too long. His almost-smile became a smirk. "Fine, yes, the rules apply to me as well." Before continuing, she ran through each point in her mind to make sure she could live with them. "Second, there will be no shenanigans."

Quinn coughed to cover up a laugh. "Shenanigans?"

"You know what I mean."

"Oh, I can guess."

Ignoring him, she held up a third finger. "You remember I am the one with the badge."

His smile vanished and he stood straight as a lance, hovering over her now at his full height. "Rule three and a half: You remember I answer to no one, not even you."

Casey scowled at him and found herself in an unpleasant quandary. "This is why I work alone." She pushed him toward the door, stooping to pick up his fallen hat during her haste, and slapped it against his chest once he was in the hallway.

"There's only the three and a half rules then?"

Her heart pounded against the inside of her chest from the exertion. She tucked her fingers in and clenched her hands into small fists. "No, just one rule now: stay away." Casey gritted out the last words and closed the door. She turned the key quickly before he thought to open it again.

She rested her forehead against the door for a full minute before turning around and sliding down until she sat on the floor with her legs splayed out on the floor in front of her. She had broken one of her cardinal rules when she let Quinn slink in and distract her—let no one interfere with the job.

Casey hoped Rose was having more luck with her case. The errant thought reminded her there was always one person she could count on for an objective opinion. She pushed herself off the floor, stripped down to her petticoat, and sat at the desk. No, she thought, a letter would not help now. Casey retrieved her journal and opened it to where she had left off earlier.

Why is he here?

She stared at the question until the words blurred into each other and then picked up her pen.

Tomorrow I will speak with Huckabee. Johnson will demand an explanation after he hears I walked out of the first meeting. There is no doubt Huckabee will whisper in someone's ear, but whose I will not yet speculate. I started work on the case tonight, doing what I always do—form background and build a foundation. Saloons are the obvious choice. Men tend to talk . . . a lot . . . when they drink or they sit in silence. Tonight, they were talking, and I thought it might have been something until the plan went sideways . . . what was Quinn doing there? Of all the saloons in this town, he happened to go to the same one at the same time . . .

Casey dropped the pen and closed the journal. Sometimes the answers one needed couldn't be found in one's thoughts, though Casey would never admit such a thing to anyone out loud.

She made use of the facility, gave herself a more thorough washing with tepid water, switched off the lights, and crawled into the comfortable bed. Sleep came in fits and starts as she played over every detail and question about the case, and no matter how hard she tried to push it out, an image of Quinn's face floated on the edges until finally, near dawn, she succumbed to slumber.

THE HAT CASEY selected to wear this morning proved useless against the sunlight beating down and causing her eyes to narrow into slits. She stood once again in front of Huckabee's brick building and ran over the impending conversation in her mind. After all, she was the one who ultimately stood in the way of Ellison Huckabee and the truth about his brother's murder.

Casey had indulged in a bath not two hours before, made possible to her specifications by offering a generous payment to Hattie, the housekeeping manager, for the inconvenience. Revived after the bath, a few stretching exercises, and a hearty breakfast with which she could find no fault, Casey was ready to face the task ahead.

She entered Huckabee's building and immediately thought two things: Linwood's face knew only one expression, and hanging would be a good way for Quinn Morgan to die. She also noticed a general bustle of activity absent from the day before.

Quinn looped his arm around her waist and whispered against her ear, "Smile, go along with it, and I will explain everything when we leave."

Their audience prevented her from jabbing her elbow into his side. "Everything?"

"I promise."

"I'm a superb shot, Quinn."

He smiled and meant it. She smiled because the alternative was to scowl and make room for questions from the secretary.

Linwood proved her wrong about having only one expression when one edge of his mouth curved, only to quickly disappear. "Mr. and Mrs. Morgan. Mr. Huckabee will see you now."

"Hanging is definitely too good for Quinn," Casey mumbled. He obviously heard her and squeezed her hand. This time when they followed Linwood down the hallway, they passed offices with men and women performing various tasks or in conversation. Once inside Huckabee's office, Casey put a few feet between her and Quinn.

"Miss McKenzie. Mr. Morgan." Huckabee gestured to the chairs in front of his desk. Neither accepted.

Casey sent Quinn an infinitesimal shake of her head, and he wisely refrained from speaking first. She spoke to the man behind the impressive mahogany desk. "I have three questions for you Mr. Huckabee, and three conditions. Once answered, and agreed upon, I promise to do all in my capability to find your brother's murderer, and if possible, locate the stolen money."

"I am only interested in finding my brother's killer, Miss McKenzie."

She waited for the lie in his statement to present itself, and when it did not, she said, "That will, of course, be my—" she held back a sigh "—*our* priority."

Huckabee agreed immediately, which put Casey on alert. She finally sat down so the men would not feel obligated to remain standing, but she took her time about it. Under usual circumstances, she would not care, and yet for reasons she could not explain, in this instance, it was important to her they understand she decides what happens next.

"WHY DO YOU trust Mr. Linwood and not your other employees?"

Quinn admired the way she pushed past the preamble. There was a lot to admire about Cassandra—no, Casey—McKenzie, and in the early hours of the morning, when she pushed him from her room, he concluded he wanted to get to know her a lot better.

Huckabee shifted a little in his seat and rested his wool-clad forearms on the desk. "I was warned to expect the unexpected about you, Miss McKenzie, and I see now why. Yes, Linwood is a trusted confidant in all matters of Huckabee Mining. I believe my employees are loyal, but since my brother met his end in this building, naturally, they fall under suspicion."

"Except Mr. Linwood."

"Yes. As it happens, he was in Denver on business."

"Where were you, Mr. Huckabee?"

Quinn enjoyed watching Casey work, though he thought she might have pushed her questioning too far. He thought to interject a qualification about standard practice, but when he caught the slight tick on the edge of Huckabee's left eye, he silently called out a "Bravo!" to Casey.

"Your second question, I presume." Huckabee cleared his throat and peeked at the closed door before replying. "I understand it is necessary to ask, but I have a condition of my own."

Casey nodded once. "Go ahead."

"Discretion. You must assure whatever I say goes no further."

"I always guarantee confidentiality, Mr. Huckabee. However, if what you have to say is of importance to the case, then I cannot make such an assurance." Casey scooted to the edge of her seat as though preparing to rise. "If you cannot live with that, then I am afraid we have nothing more to discuss."

Quinn stood at the same time as Casey, more to see what she would do next than for solidarity. She started for the door when Huckabee said, "Very well." He waved in frustration at the chairs again. Once seated, he continued. "I have been happily married for fifteen years."

"I see."

"You aren't going to write this down, are you?"

Casey tapped the side of her head. "There is no need. Please, continue."

"I was with . . . another woman the night my brother died, and I will forever regret my folly. I should have been here, I know." Huckabee held a hand pressed to his heart.

"Regret does no good in these situations, Mr. Huckabee." Casey did not blink, smirk, or ask for more details about the mistress.

"You might be right, Miss McKenzie." Huckabee gave her a smile like one an indulgent father might offer a child. "You have one more question, do you not?"

"Will you and Linwood protect our ruse no matter what we might say or do?"

Huckabee blinked twice in between a glance between Quinn and Casey. "You are asking for a lot of latitude."

"It is, but it is also necessary."

"Do you have anything to add?"

Quinn shook his head. "Miss McKenzie speaks for us both." He caught the slight slump in her shoulders when she released some of the stiffness from her back. "Consider whatever she asks a question from me as well."

Huckabee intertwined his fingers and returned a thoughtful gaze to Casey. "You have my word."

Casey stood once more, surprising the men. Quinn waited for Huckabee to ask the question they must both be thinking, and the predictable man did not disappoint.

"You had three conditions, Miss McKenzie."

Her half-smile remained firmly in place as she replied, "Consider them met, Mr. Huckabee."

CHAPTER 10

Quinn cradled Casey's arm and steered her toward a nearby stockyard. Wind blew at the edges of her hat, forcing her to hold on to it with one hand. He kept his in place as a cool breeze whipped around and faded behind them. A layer of gray clouds cast shadows on the earth as they danced with the sun, allowing light to sneak through on the occasional rotation.

"Where are we going?"

He peered down at her. "That's all you have to ask?"

"I thought it best to yell at you *after* we got to where we're going."

"Do you ever tire of wanting to yell at people?"

"Since you are the only one—"

"I've got it." Quinn stopped a short distance from a stockyard worker. "Do you have a carriage or wagon for rent?"

The worker fetched his manager, who called him by name. "You're wanting your horse, Mr. Morgan?"

"Not this time, Mr. Adams. A carriage for today." The

manager took in their fine clothes, spending a few seconds longer looking over Cassandra, before naming a price. Quinn did not think twice before handing over what amounted to twice what it should cost. "We'll return it in two hours."

The manager grinned and sent his young worker off to hitch a carriage. He returned with a team of two tall and handsome bays pulling a black Studebaker carriage with red padded seats. It was not the most practical choice, but Quinn still preferred horses to horseless vehicles.

"Owner sold it before he left on the train ahead of last winter," Mr. Adams said by way of explanation. "Fool city folks never learn."

Quinn did not offer a reply. Once they were seated, and he had control of the reins, Casey readjusted a hairpin so her hat remained in place. "Huckabee is lying."

"I know." He set the horses in motion onto a road leading out of town and followed the river. Twenty minutes of silence later, save for flowing water and occasional birdsong, he stopped the horses on a flat expanse near an embankment. Mountains rolled above the winding river, and the darker clouds remained at a distance for now. The clean bouquet of woodsy pine scented the air and a watery freshness indicated impending snow or rain. Quinn did not care which, and only hoped the weather held long enough for them to do what had to be done.

He climbed down and offered a hand up to her. After a moment's hesitation, she placed her hand in his, then gave a small yelp when he instead splayed his strong hands around her waist and lifted her down.

Casey swatted at his hand even after he released her. "Rule two: No shenanigans."

Quinn smiled in response. "Your last rule was to stay away, which made me think the others no longer applied."

"You have an obnoxious lawyerly way of twisting what one says to suit your purposes."

"Somehow I think you are about to use that to suit *your* purposes."

Casey shrugged.

"What were the three conditions for Huckabee?" Quinn slowed the horses down a little with a gentle pull of the reins.

"Do they matter when he agreed to them?"

"He didn't."

"He did, when he asked me to take the case."

"You don't have any." Quinn chuckled. "You realize he is probably in his office still thinking about what conditions he agreed to."

"I know. It helps to keep them wondering."

"Them?"

"Clients, about how far I will go and what I will demand of them."

Quinn slowed the team a little more as they reached their destination. "What would you have done if he pressed the issue?"

"No one ever has, but I would have come up with a few." Casey glanced at him over her shoulder. She stretched her legs for the short distance to where water met earth and watched the gentle flow.

"What are we doing out here?"

"A better question is why did you willingly come along?"

"I trust you."

"While I am curious how you determined my trustworthiness so soon in our acquaintance, I'll leave it for now to answer your question." Quinn spread his arms wide as though embracing the landscape. "There is no one else here."

"You dislike people?"

"Not as rule, no. I think you might be of a similar sentiment."

Casey regarded him carefully and grudgingly concluded that perhaps they had more in common than she would like to admit aloud. Commonalities bred intimacy, and she could not afford it right now. "Whether or not I am, you at least picked a lovely spot."

It was time to return to the reason they were both there. "Huckabee is lying," she said again, "but I do not think he killed his brother, and he has no reason to steal his own money." She waited a few seconds to add, "He is right not to trust his employees."

"I agree, but why do you think so?"

"It is obvious that someone working in the building, or at least someone with access, played a part in both the murder *and* the theft. Considering the care he took with security on the front of the building, I assume the back is just as protected. We'll have to verify."

"But it is a safe assumption." Quinn removed his hat to let the sun touch his face. "However, the two crimes don't fit together."

"No, they do not." Casey leaned down to pick up a smooth pebble and turn it over in her gloved hand, revealing rough edges where it had crusted with dirt and frost over time. "What if they are connected? One intentional and one an accident?"

"You are jumping over a lot of supposition and straight to a conclusion that has no proof."

She dropped the stone and tilted her head back slightly to peer at him from beneath her hat. "Are you a lawyer or a bounty hunter on this case?"

"You don't like either, so does it matter?"

She held back a smile. "It does. I'd have to adjust my thinking for a lawyer. A bounty hunter would understand what I meant."

Quinn chuckled and picked up the same rock she had dropped a minute ago. "Both of who I am knows what you meant, Casey, but smooth or rough, you will need proof."

"To win a case or collect a bounty, yes, and don't call me Casey."

"You already gave leave to do so."

"I have changed my mind."

"Miss McKenzie is too formal when it is just us two, now that we are friends." He handed her the rock, smooth side up. "You also need proof to make an arrest. I worked with a Pinkerton once before—I was acting as a lawyer at the time—and his creative thinking nearly got my client killed."

"We are not quite friends, and I imagine you have had to employ imaginative measures to reach your desired results. No one is perfect, *Quinn*, not even agents of the Pinkerton Detective Agency."

He made a sound she could only compare to a *harrumph* and took the rock back from her. "This stone has two sides, and each one tells a story. Using your analogy, the smooth side represents the premeditated act of stealing the money. The rough side is messy and unpredictable—the murder."

Casey smirked at him. "Correct, though I believe I already concluded as much."

His mocking gaze said more than his next words. "Allow me to work through this in a more lawyerly manner. Now, this theory makes little sense based on the timeline."

"True." Casey considered the other options and dismissed two before returning to an earlier statement. "Huckabee is lying about where he was the night of the murder, and it would be almost impossible to fake the time of death—"

"But not the theft."

"There are witnesses."

His brow raised in question before he got out, "Are there?"

Casey's experience with cursing had more to do with wishing excruciating pain on horrible people rather than the method of using profanity to make a point, but she was on the verge of doing both now. "Agent Johnson—"

"The man I saw you with in the restaurant in Colorado Springs?"

Her eyes narrowed, but she let it go for now. "Yes. He said the witness was of no value. The report he provided listed one name, but what if the person—"

"Was willing to lie?"

"Good grief, that is an annoying habit."

Quinn shrugged by way of apology. "Am I wrong?"

She did not care if her unladylike sigh would cause Mrs. Pennyworth to scold. The feisty housekeeper was in Denver, where Casey wished to be right now. The dark clouds of earlier moved beyond them, allowing sunlight to gloss over the green mountainside and emblazon the yellow aspens staggered across the landscape. Quiet and beauty warred for first prize in this place far removed from the city. Denver could wait, she decided. "Your prescience aside, it will be beneficial to our continued working relationship if you allowed me to finish a thought."

"I can agree to that."

"How very accommodating of you." Casey brushed a bit of dirt from her gloves and listened to a new wave of thunder snarling in the distance. The expected crack rent the air a few seconds later, though she did not see the lightning. "It sounds like we are to get rain instead of snow. Pity." Facing Quinn, she spoke her next thought. "Now, if the witness lied—"

"Supposition at this point."

Her snarl nearly matched the thunder.

Quinn held up both hands in surrender. "It seems to be an affliction."

"Then find a cure. As I was saying, if the witness lied, either Huckabee or someone else must have paid handsomely. It would not have been a simple thing to lie to the marshal."

"Unless the marshal is in on it."

"I have not yet met Marshal Wickline, but from what I have learned, he is an honest lawman."

"When did you have time to look into the town marshal?"

Exasperated, Casey lifted her skirt only enough to walk back through tall grass on her way to the carriage. "You wanted me to yell after we were far away from town, and now I fully understand that with you, yelling is a foregone conclusion."

"Or an affliction."

Casey stopped halfway to the carriage. "I brought my gun."

His eyes roamed over her entire body. "It is unkind to tease a man's imagination."

"I give up." Casey picked up her skirts again and walked. "I visited more than a saloon since our arrival," she said when he matched her step.

Quinn reached the carriage ahead of her. "So did I, and it turns out the marshal was not in Durango the nights of either the theft or the murder."

Well hell, Casey thought. She had not heard about the

marshal's absence, and it galled her to think he had learned more in the short time since their arrival. "Fine, he was not here, but that does not mean he played a role in either incident. For now, I am giving him the benefit of his good name."

The first tiny drops of rain fell from the darkening sky. Quinn helped her into the carriage and appreciated the covering as the rain continued. The horses easily navigated the hard-packed earth, not yet muddied.

"You didn't yell."

"The rain interrupted my plans. Yours, too, I imagine. What was the purpose of dragging me out to the river, only to return so quickly?"

"As you said, the rain interrupted plans."

They pulled into the stockyard soon after the drops turned to hard pellets, and Quinn steered the animals to a tall overhang attached to the livery building.

He left Casey in the carriage long enough to speak with the stockyard manager. "How much for exclusive use while I am in town?"

Mr. Adams eyed him as though he found a naïve city gent he could take for another exorbitant rate. He named a price.

"You can do better."

"Exclusive use?"

"Yes," Quinn confirmed. "And I want the horses stabled and groomed."

Mr. Adams sighed and named another rate, not much more

reasonable than the last. Quinn retrieved his pocketbook, withdrew a few bills, and held them just above the manager's hand. "The carriage and those horses are easy to spot. Do not think you can swindle me and rent them out to someone else."

"You've my word."

Quinn passed the man the bills. "You will receive the second half of the fee before I leave town. If such an arrangement makes you nervous, you may ask after me at Huckabee Mining."

The man quickly tucked the bills into his pocket and shook his head. "Reckon that's as good a reference as someone can get in this town, less, of course, you know Marshal Wickline. Ain't no better word than his or Mr. Huckabee's. Shame about his brother."

"Do you know the marshal?" Casey asked from the carriage. She had scooted over to the driver's side.

"I plan to drive you back to the hotel and then return here."

"Seems you would have thought of that sooner," she whispered for him alone.

Quinn sent her a scathing look only she could see. He swore he saw her stick her tongue out at him. Ignoring it for now, he helped her down but kept her close. She did not appear to mind the mud forming in the yard.

"Sure. Everyone in town knows the marshal." He tsked and looked back at Quinn as though Casey didn't know what she was talking about. "My word is good."

"Excellent. Stabled and groomed. Don't forget." Quinn had

already paid him handsomely to stable and care for his horse, so he had no reason not to trust the man.

The manager tapped the edge of his hat, and after darting a few glances between the covered area where the horses now stood and the pummeling rain, he yelled for his younger worker to unhitch the horses.

Satisfied the man meant to keep his word, Quinn shrugged out of his jacket.

"What are you doing? You'll soak through between here and the hotel."

"I was trying to be a gentleman. I assure you there is not an umbrella hiding beneath this duster. There is still time to drive you over."

"I'd rather we get soaked than those beautiful animals." She helped pull his jacket back on. "Your chivalry is appreciated and noted, but there is no sense in it. Either way, I will want a long, hot bath, so how wet I become does not matter."

They heard a loud chuckle behind them. Casey and Quinn both looked, but the manager was next to the carriage, whistling and not looking in their direction.

Casey checked to make sure her hat was still secure, and she did not argue when Quinn pulled her close to his side. His larger body provided some protection from the weather, and lifting the hem of her skirt so it did not skim the mud, she leaned up and whispered, "You are a most aggravating husband."

CHAPTER 11

No act of God or man could make Casey regret asking the housekeeping staff for enough water to fill the big tub in front of the woodstove. She slinked down until the water lapped beneath her neck, which left her knees exposed, but she took care of that by occasionally splashing water over them. Her current state of contentment almost made up for it not being the oversized porcelain tub at the Denver house.

Wind rattled the rain-battered windows, yet the effect did more to comfort than cause concern. Storms were not uncommon across Colorado's expanse of mountains and plains, but it had been years since the area flooded, so Casey preferred not to worry about such things unless they happened.

Even as she watched, the thick drops pounding against the windows shifted to silent brushes of snow, which lasted only a few minutes before dissipating. Darkness won in the end as the sky quieted and boisterous parts of town awakened. Casey would have remained in the bath for another hour had the water not cooled. Even the warmth from the woodstove could not heat it enough to convince her to remain submerged. She reached for the linen towel she had placed on a chair near the stove to warm and wrapped it around herself as she rose and shivered against the sudden rush of air on her skin.

She tucked one end of the towel beneath her arm, wishing it covered more of her body, then Casey stilled. The knock came again, and this time there was no mistaking it was at her door. "I swear I'm going to kill him." Casey stepped out of the tub but held off on ringing for housekeeping again. They could deal with the water later. "Go away," she called out. When Quinn did not respond, Casey walked a little closer to the door. "Quinn?"

The knob rattled subtly but enough for Casey to notice. She quickly donned her nightgown and robe as a quiet scratching came from the other side of the door near the lock. She grabbed her Colt from the top of the dresser, and on bare feet, moved toward the door. Thinking she'd rather face whoever was on the other side than have them push their way in, Casey flattened herself against the wall as much as possible, reached for the lock, and twisted the key. With a quick flick, she turned the knob.

Before she could scream, yell, or fire her pistol, a man she'd never seen before slammed against the wall and flailed half in and half out of the room. He spun around and connected his fist to Quinn's face before Quinn returned the favor, though Quinn's punch landed the stranger against the opposite wall where he slumped to the floor.

Casey leaned her head into the hall and noticed a few other guests were doing the same. They weren't in a part of town that would normally lend itself to a ruckus. Of course, if she believed what she had heard about the proprietress and the entertainment girls on the top floor, she could believe anything happening there.

Quinn looked pointedly in her direction. He did not sound out of breath, though he rubbed the top of his hand. "Be a dear and fetch something I can use to tie him up."

The audience—and curiosity—prevented Casey from doing what she wanted to, so she went back into the room and returned fifteen seconds later with a pair of Bean handcuffs. His infernal brow raised when he accepted them from her, but he had little trouble getting them on the culprit since they were conveniently unlocked.

"Remind me to get those back when he's handed off to the sheriff. It's the only pair I brought with me." Casey stepped back and closed the door, leaving Quinn to deal with the sheriff and onlookers.

As much as she would like to have questioned both Quinn and the man who tried to enter her room, her nightclothes would have drawn far too much speculation. After changing into a simple skirt and shirt and the woolen sweater Mrs. Pennyworth had given her five years ago at Christmas, she slipped her boots on without stockings, slid the blade into its sheath, and returned to the hallway to find Quinn at the landing next to the stairs speaking with a man whose face she could not see.

She fought against instinct and held her temper when she noticed the grim expression Quinn wore as he parted ways with the man. Frustration and concern were both etched beneath what she thought looked to be exhaustion. "What happened, and who was he?"

"May we speak inside?"

Casey left him to follow, and once he had the door closed, he waited several seconds before walking any farther into the room. He set her handcuffs on the dresser.

"Were you going out?"

She peered down at her casual attire and then back at him. "Only to find you and ask after the man. What happened, Quinn?" His name slipped naturally from her lips, as though she had spoken it a million times before. "I didn't recognize him."

"He's not known in these parts." He looked at the chair by the stove. "May I?"

Casey nodded, concerned more now because of his overly polite behavior. "Where is he known?"

"He's wanted in Virginia and South Carolina, but he's only recently come this far west." Quinn leaned into the back of the chair. "Sheriff Aircy recognized him from a new batch of posters he received last week. His name is Burton Amos."

Extracting information out of Quinn was worse than a visit to the dentist. "What is he wanted for?"

"Rape and murder."

Casey sat on the bed and stared at Quinn. "He wouldn't have done either. I was armed."

"I do not doubt your ability to take care of yourself, nor do I doubt he would have tried both."

"Why me? There are easier targets outside the hotel." Casey went to the washstand and poured water from the pitcher into the only clean glass and handed it to Quinn before she sat back on the bed. "I have nothing stronger."

Quinn's smile didn't light his eyes. "This'll do, but I do not require consoling. As to why you, he wouldn't say. The sheriff thought it's likely he saw you about, and Amos decided to . . . well . . ."

"I don't believe that any more than you do. Men like him are rarely selective. I know because I've brought a few in, and they'll go after just about anyone in a skirt. It's too coincidental for him to be in Durango at the same time we're here at Huckabee's request."

"I agree." Quinn rubbed a hand over his dark, trimmed beard. "There's a hefty bounty on his head, and they'll send him back east for trial."

"That should be your bounty." Casey rejected the uneasy reaction in her stomach to the possibility that Quinn would be the one to deliver Burton Amos. She'd solved dozens of cases on her own before, and she'd solve a dozen more after he left.

"I'm already on a case; one I believe is infinitely more

interesting and important. Amos will get whatever is coming to him no matter who brings him in, and the bounty doesn't interest me. I'm more concerned about why he was in Durango. As you said, it's too coincidental."

"Yes, it is." Something about the way Quinn kept looking at her prompted her to ask, "What brought you to my door tonight? You couldn't have known he was trying to get in."

"Chance. I was coming over to ask if you wanted to accompany me to dinner. I found him instead."

"Fortuitous." Casey regarded him with a few sideways glances. The shift to another subject gave them both a chance to ponder their own thoughts about Amos before they did too much speculating. A lot of wanted men ventured west hoping to escape into the mountains. Perhaps Amos was just another one of many. "Thank you. As to supper, I had hoped to convince the hotel to send something up. Does the manager know what happened here tonight?"

"Miss Mashburn wanted an explanation when the sheriff arrived. She was more concerned about one of her guests having an unpleasant experience. I assured her no harm came to you."

Casey plucked at her skirt and thought of her rumbling stomach. "If you give me a few minutes, I will dress properly and we can go down to eat. I suppose people will need to see us socially if the ruse is to work."

Quinn found his smile again. "Before, at the stockyard, you called me a 'most aggravating husband.' Now, how are you to know that when we've been married only a day?"

"It doesn't take much to keep your spirits up, does it?" Casey waved him toward the door. "Tomorrow will be soon enough for me to want to yell at you again. Right now, I am hungry, and the relaxing effects of my bath have worn off."

Mention of the bath brought Quinn's eyes to the brass tub. "They wouldn't bring a tub and hot water to my room."

"I paid them generously for it, and Miss Mashburn didn't hide her smile when she named a price, but it was worth it."

Quinn's face possessed a myriad of expressions, and Casey was already getting good at figuring out which one went with the corresponding mood or emotion, at least until he came up with a new one she hadn't seen . . . like now.

"What is that look for?"

"I have some knowledge of a Pinkerton's salary, and I have seen some of what you keep in the trunk you carry around."

"What I do with my money is none of your business." She reverted to proper address to annoy him and to steady herself because he was acting like a husband or family, and she couldn't decide, which riled her more.

"True, but if our ruse, as you keep calling it, is to work, then we should at least know the basics about one another."

"Fine." Casey glanced at the presentable dress she withdrew from her trunk, and once again silently praised Mrs. Pennyworth's lessons on how to prevent wrinkles. They didn't always work, but Casey blamed a rumpled wardrobe on hasty packing habits rather than the housekeeper's efforts. "Wait outside and we will discuss it over the meal."

"Tell me one thing I don't know about you, and the rest can wait."

Quinn remained in place, but Casey felt his warmth from across the room's short length, or did the heat come from within? She wouldn't be able to answer that question until he left.

"Very well. I do not live off my salary alone. For the purposes of our charade, you will play the lawyer, which should not be difficult given it is true, and I will play the part of your spoiled wife who has a firm grasp of business matters."

He chuckled. "Given this some thought, have you?"

"Not as much as you have." She gestured to the door. "Now go. I will only need a few minutes."

True to her word, Casey emerged less than ten minutes later. She had learned long ago to style her hair simply, yet respectably, for most social situations. She lacked the skill to completely subdue every soft curl or wayward strand, but Casey never gave much thought to her appearance, except when it came to putting on a show to solve a case . . . until now.

Irked with herself for caring what Quinn might think of her looks—good or bad—she deemed her hair and clothes presentable enough to dine out in Durango. Apparently, she did more than well enough if she was reading Quinn's newest expression correctly. He did not comment, though, except to ask, "However did you manage without assistance?"

"I suppose you would have offered."

He smiled. "It is appropriate for a husband to help his wife in whatever she requires."

"If the wife is accommodating, which this one is not." She stopped him before they descended the stairs. "Tell me something about yourself I don't already know. One thing and the rest can wait."

Quinn took his time considering before his lips spread into a wider grin. "I have never been married, until now, of course."

Casey hardly considered that worthy of a confession, but she was oddly pleased by it. "You're not married now. You are, however, a scoundrel."

"All right." He cupped her elbow and started down the stairs, keeping her close enough so he could whisper. They passed a single man and another couple on the way down, and once alone again, he said, "You asked me before why I wanted to work with you."

"Yes, and your responses were glib."

"Do you want to hear this or not?"

Casey's head titled back and studied him a little closer, curious about the accent she briefly detected, yet leaving it alone for now. "Yes, I do."

"You won't like it."

"I assume not."

"Protection."

"I am going to hope, and assume, you mean protection for yourself."

Quinn gave her an exasperated look. "Assume all you want. We have already been told more than one lie, and that was before we have even delved into the case. I don't trust Huckabee nor your Agent Johnson."

"I hope you do not think I am surprised by your declaration."

"You're not?"

"You are a man, and most men of good upbringing and believers in chivalry cannot help themselves." She disengaged her elbow from his hand. "This all brings up a more pressing point, and one I did not consider fully when I agreed."

"And you called *me* aggravating." Quinn raised his eyes heavenward. "What is this pressing point?"

"We are in separate rooms."

"Easily rectified."

"And we will remain in separate rooms."

"You do cut a man to the quick."

Casey proceeded down the last few steps before turning back around. She wished she hadn't, for now, Quinn had an even greater height advantage. She returned to the step where he stood, then gave herself a more favored position by gaining one more step so she could face him eye to eye. "Can you not be serious?"

He proved he could by snaking an arm around her waist and pulling her close. To anyone who might happen upon them, they appeared a most loving couple in an embrace too intimate for public display. She felt his warm breath on her face, and his mouth hovered mere inches away when he spoke again. "Don't look now, my dear, but our drunken friend from Colorado Springs is at the front desk."

CHAPTER 12

Quinn held her close, his arm tight enough around her waist to prevent her from stepping away, but not so tight she could not leave his embrace if she chose. The drunkard had gotten a good look at them both the night of the wagon explosion, though she doubted he would remember them.

Casey was hardly forgettable wearing a duster over her nightclothes and yelling at the man as though she alone had the power to bring holy hell down upon his head. Yes, she would have made a memorable impression, regardless of the man's intoxicated state.

"Are you certain it is him?"

Quinn nodded and shifted her a little so she stood on the step below and kept his face partially hidden. "It's him."

"People travel from one railroad town to the next all the time. What makes him seem suspicious?"

A smartly dressed man passed them, and Quinn said nothing until he was out of hearing range. "He's speaking with one of the clerks I saw at Huckabee's office."

Casey started to turn around, but Quinn tightened his grip a fraction.

"This is ridiculous, Quinn. Release me now so we can go to dinner."

Surprised at her blasé attitude, he shifted his focus back to her face. "You don't find it curious?"

"Of course I do, but standing here like this is more suspicious than if we go about our business as any normal couple would. The clerk—if he noticed us at all—would have seen us together. The drunk fool saw us together. However, if he remembers anything, it will probably be you pulling me away from him, which is something a husband would do."

"As usual, you have oversimplified a situation. If you think that man does not remember you clearly in the state of undress you were at the time, then you are as much a fool as him."

Casey pressed the heel of her boot into the toe of his. He grimaced only slightly, which he would congratulate himself for later. The woman knew exactly where to apply the right amount of pressure.

"Are we going to dinner together, or am I going alone?"

Quinn cleared his throat and set her gently away from him. He held out an arm and relaxed when she looped her arm through it. "Some men might call you a shrew."

"You wouldn't?"

He kept a straight face. "I care too much for living to test it."

She laughed then, a soft sound that drew a few approving glances in her direction, including the drunk. The man stared for a few seconds then looked at his companion.

"Our friend is leaving."

"So I see." Once outside, Casey tugged on his arm. "We're going this way."

"The restaurant I had in mind is in the other direction."

"Yes, but—"

"Don't even think it." Quinn pulled her into the shadows, a place he seemed to spend a lot of time since meeting her. "I'm not taking you into a potential confrontation."

"I told you before, this is what I do." She pushed him away. "If you can't accept that, then we can't work together."

Quinn swore under his breath and refused to apologize. "All right, but I'm the only one with a gun right now." He looked her over top to bottom. "You're carrying one, aren't you?"

"If you have to ask . . ."

Intense curiosity consumed him as he thought about where she might keep it. He had not felt a gun when he held her close, which made him think she strapped it to her leg, and that aroused images better left restrained.

They continued walking, appearing like any other couple out for a stroll or on their way to or from the evening meal. It was half-past seven in the evening, and gone were the clouds and signs of a storm. The proud display of stars dimmed for nothing except the bright yellow moon.

Every time the crescent's light touched the edges of Casey's hair, the copper hues brightened against the darker browns and reds. Perhaps she was right, Quinn thought, they shouldn't work together. He wanted to, and he believed it was better for them and the case, but she was also too much of a distraction, proven when she mentioned their quarry had veered down another street and Quinn didn't notice.

"You will look too out of place in that part of town unless, of course, you want to go back to the hotel and dress in those boy's duds you wore to the saloon."

She gave the thought some consideration.

"I don't think so." He leaned closer. "Besides, our friend has met up with the clerk again."

Down the alley, on the other side of the buildings, the light was faint, but the two men were clearly visible. "What are the chances," Casey began, "our drunk imbecile from Colorado Springs was drunk?"

"We both smelled the alcohol on him."

"Yes, and I smelled it on his breath, too, but drunkenness can be faked. What if blowing up that wagon was intentional?"

Quinn eased her back so the two men wouldn't notice her hair if the moonlight touched it again. He peered around the corner. "To what end? There wasn't a crime committed, at least not that the sheriff mentioned. You think he was part of the robbery?"

"Not necessarily."

When he pulled back, he studied Casey, who appeared lost in deliberation. "What then?"

"Think like a lawyer, Quinn." Casey held a hand over her stomach when it rumbled. "We really should have dinner."

"The lawyer in me would speculate that our gun-powder igniting friend is for hire, and his arrival in Durango is not directly linked to either the robbery or murder but could be linked to the cover-up."

"I agree—mostly." Casey yanked on a piece of Quinn's sleeve. "I need to eat."

Quinn spoke through his teeth and restrained from throttling her. "The lawyer in me would also consider the other option."

"Which is?"

"He's a drunk imbecile who accidentally blew up a wagon, and might I add, that is the more likely scenario."

"Everyone is a suspect, Quinn. Everyone."

"You said you wanted to follow him."

Her shoulders rose and fell in a dainty shrug. "You said we weren't going to, and he's not going anywhere tonight. Now, where is that restaurant?"

CASEY UNLOCKED HER hotel room door and stopped just beneath the threshold. Light from the hall drifted in and the open curtains allowed enough moonlight through the windows to illuminate the room. Seconds later, Quinn's tall frame cast a shadow on the wall.

"Someone knows why we are here."

Quinn gently moved her aside and walked into the room first. "Or there is a thief in the hotel ransacking rooms."

"Were your belongings rifled through?"

"I didn't get as far as unlocking my door when I saw you standing in yours."

Casey surveyed the mess. "Those yellow-bellied, good-for-nothings destroyed my trunk."

"I'd wager you know a lot of inappropriate words when the occasion calls for it. It looks like it can be repaired. Did you have any money in here?"

Casey nodded and walked to the trunk. She pulled out everything inside, felt along the edges of the inside base, and lifted the back right corner. "It is still here."

Quinn stood over her. "Clever, and thankfully your intruders were not."

She crossed the room to the bureau and opened the top drawer. "They took the purse I kept in here, but there wasn't much."

"A diversion then?"

"You've never employed it yourself?"

"I don't leave money in my room." Quinn patted his jacket over his chest. "And no one has been foolish enough to relieve me of what I carry."

Casey surveyed the rest of the mess, from her clothes strewn about to the mattress half on, half off the bed frame, and the water pitcher broken in half a dozen pieces on the floor next to the washstand. It appeared the curtains were the only items not disturbed by the frenzied and destructive search.

"You'll need another room tonight."

"I can clean this mess." Casey did not relish doing so, but neither did she want anyone else in there.

Quinn moved closer. "You won't sleep well knowing what's happened in here."

He was right, of course. Casey counted herself lucky that the thieves did not appear to have damaged her clothes. Another thought shot through her mind, and she hurried to the washstand and opened the cupboard. She knelt on the floor and twisted on all fours until she could see underneath.

"What are you doing?"

A sigh of relief escaped her lips when she removed the journal from where she had wedged it between the bowl and the piece of wood beneath it. She held it up for him to see. "My journal."

Quinn helped her to her feet. "You went to a lot of trouble to hide it."

"I write case notes in here."

"Have you written about this case?"

Casey thought of the combination of case-related thoughts mixed in with a few about Quinn and nodded. "Not much yet."

"As a lawyer, I applaud you for keeping a written record. However, under the circumstances, please refrain from writing anything else down while we're here, or at least allow me to—"

She pulled it back from his outstretched hand. "No. I will simply have to keep it with me."

"Is there something in there I shouldn't see, Miss McKenzie?"

Casey pressed the journal close to her chest. "Am I going to have to stop trusting you, Mr. Morgan?"

His grin always disarmed her. "On my honor, I will not give you cause."

"Good." Casey tucked the journal in her reticule and frowned at the odd shape it created. She moved it to her valise, all the while thinking she should burn it. "Now, if you will leave me to clean this mess, I will see you in the morning."

Quinn stopped her from moving the mattress by herself. "I'm going to have another room prepared for you, and the hotel can take care of the cleaning. If you gather your clothes and other items, I will see to your trunk when I return."

He left no room for argument or negotiation, and in his arrogant manner, expected her to do as instructed. Casey reverted to the lowliest days of her youth and stuck her tongue out at his departing back. When he chuckled, she drew her tongue back and clamped her mouth shut. It took a few mental reminders that he couldn't have seen her, which meant he predicted her indignation and didn't expect her to do any of what she said.

It was lowering to think he already knew her so well.

She pushed, tugged, and shoved the mattress until it was back in place. With hands on hips and a single, jerky nod, Casey smiled at her unnecessary act of rebellion, if for no other reason than to prove she took orders from no one, except the Pinkerton Agency. Her arrogance now deflated, she gathered each item removed from the trunk, smoothed every article of clothing out the best she could, and packed them all away again.

By the time Quinn returned with a key to another room, she was ready to leave and silently grateful for it. It was only the second time in her career that one of her hotel rooms had been robbed, but the first time she had *wanted* it to happen. Undercover as a wealthy widow, her plan to catch a group of young out-of-work cowboys preying on single women of means had succeeded. She caught them in the act, they confessed to their crimes, and she moved onto the next case.

This time, however, made little sense. She was traveling light, with only one trunk and a valise, and her clothing, while fine, was not extraordinary. What other reason did they have to rummage through her belongings unless they were a part of whatever was happening at Huckabee Mining Company?

Quinn noted the mattress and kept a smile from forming. "You've been busy." He held up the new key and pressed it in her open palm. "Miss Mashburn will not be charging you for your stay in this room."

Casey stared at the key, then looked up at him. "However did you manage such a feat? The woman strikes me as someone who prefers to receive a dollar rather than give up a penny."

"She's a reasonable woman and knows that keeping her guests happy means greater profits in the future." Quinn lifted one end of the trunk, twisted his arm a little, and heaved it up onto his back. "Ready?"

She realized he had caught her staring and shook herself from the stupor. "Yes." Casey picked up her valise and reticule and closed the door once they were both in the hallway. "Which way?"

"Follow me."

Less than five seconds later, Quinn stopped and moved aside so she could use the key. She looked up at the room number then at his face. "Do you mean to say the only other room available in this hotel is the one right next to yours?"

CHAPTER 13

Renowned lock picker Alfred C. Hobbs she was not, and while Casey considered herself an unlikely apprentice of his work, she thought even he could find little to criticize with her entry into the Huckabee Mining Company office building. Although, he would no doubt have been able to gain entry in half the time she had managed.

Casey scanned the area behind the large, brick building one more time before slipping in through the back door and softly closing it behind her. She navigated through a back hall until she found the one leading to Ellison's office. Her elbow bumped a panel on the wall, and a hollow echo returned.

"What have you been up to, Mr. Huckabee?"

With the tips of her fingers, she felt along the edges but found no latch or lever. She pushed against it, again to no avail. Casey gave up in favor of finding Frank Huckabee's office. She doubted Ellison would have cleared it out so soon after his brother's death, if not for sentimental reasons, then for appearances. A search of the entire floor did not reveal an office that could have belonged to the deceased Huckabee.

She returned to Ellison's office, made quicker work of the lock than she had with the back door, and gave her eyes a minute to adjust to the brighter space. Moonlight filtered in through the top section of two windows not covered by curtains. Casey stood near the door and attempted to figure out why everything about the room appeared off. Nothing looked different from her first two visits, yet the space seemed to close in on her now.

She visualized the hallway in which she entered and how it laid out in relation to the office in the far right wall. "Why, you cagey man." Casey spent the next twenty minutes studying every foot of the wall before she found the seam. She removed a painting from the wood paneling and discovered a hidden lever beneath. A light tug was all the lever needed, and the door opened.

"What are you doing?"

Had she not heard the amusement in his voice or recognized the deep timbre even in a whisper, she might have expired on the spot or at the least, suffered a debilitating heart attack. As it happened, her heart's beat increased its pace. Her eyes pinched together as she silently cursed, then followed with a quiet apology.

"What are *you* doing?"

"Following you."

Casey shook her head. "Not possible. I know when someone

is following me, and no one was."

"Think of it then as anticipating you."

"You think you know me so well?"

Quinn's raised a brow in response to her question.

"Fine. Be quiet and don't get in my way." She took in his black clothing on his tall frame. "Even in those clothes, you're too big to move about unnoticed."

His cocky grin widened. "And yet, you did not notice me."

Casey entered the space on the other side of the wall and closed the portal behind her. When he said something about his finger, she smiled and proceeded up the stairs. As she reached the second floor of the building through the hidden staircase, one question tumbled over and over in her mind. "Why, Mr. Huckabee, was there a need to hide this staircase when both lead to the same floor?"

"You don't expect an answer, do you?"

"If I did, I would not have asked a man who was not here." She did not bother to turn around when Quinn joined her. Even moving quietly on the steps, she heard his ascent and arrival.

"Do you always talk to yourself?"

Casey shrugged. "You don't?"

The dark corridor they found themselves in was not as dusty as one might expect, and a thin stream of light beneath a section of the wall guided them. The lack of light prevented Casey from seeing where she touched, and after a few minutes, her eyes still had not adjusted enough to see beyond her nose.

"If I won't be too much in your way, may I try?"

Quinn stood close enough to her that Casey had to step back to breathe. "By all means." She waved her hand toward the wall knowing he couldn't see it. She heard his fingers move along the wood, then heard a latch click. The portal swung open.

She nearly fell into the room hoping to breathe fresher air. Instead, she sucked in a bit of dust and coughed it back out. Even in the dim room, a quick perusal revealed at least a month's worth of dust on every surface. "This can't be Frank Huckabee's office. He hasn't been dead long enough for it to be in such a state."

Quinn brushed particles from his long jacket. "You thought the staircase would lead to Frank's office?"

"I expected it to lead somewhere important, but on the other side of that door is the rest of the floor and probably more offices. Why hide it?" Casey walked to the built-in shelves and scanned the hardbound books but found nothing of interest. Most did not appear to have been read recently, if at all.

She moved then to the desk where Quinn was looking but not touching. "Anything important?"

Quinn pointed to an envelope on top of a stack of loose papers. "Depends on what you define as important."

Casey reached for it before pulling her hand back. "It has not been there as long as all this dust."

"No, it hasn't." He picked up the envelope, flipped it over, and lifted the open flap. "It's not sealed."

"Whoever put it there will know someone handled it."

"You made certain to get permission from Huckabee for anything you might do or need. He didn't know the extent to which you'd go, but let us not be hypocrites." Quinn removed the single half-sheet of paper from the envelope. "Interesting."

"What is?"

He handed it to her. "It's interesting that it *isn't* interesting." Quinn walked to the door and found it barred from the inside. "They didn't want anyone in here, and the bar explains the hidden access to this room. No window between here and the rooms on the other side."

Casey put the letter back and replaced the envelope in the same place where its impression remained on the dusty papers. "Stands to reason we are in the right place."

"Yes, but Frank Huckabee wasn't killed in this room." Quinn removed the bar and opened the door. He did not make it far into the next room and asked over his shoulder, "What details were you given about Frank's death?"

She came up behind him and peered around his right side. "Not much, and I didn't ask. I prefer to investigate and draw my own conclusions." Casey brushed by him and looked around at the large, communal work area for the employees. Two rows of tables took up the center of the room, and shelves lined an entire wall on one side. The opposite side boasted a map of Colorado that took up almost half the space, and next to it was a long line of drawers built beneath open shelves.

Every surface, including the floor, appeared free of dirt, grime, or anything else that might interfere with daily work. Writing utensils and tidy stacks of blank paper sat in the center of each table.

"It's too clean. There isn't even the slightest smell of anything in the air except a little beeswax, probably to polish the floors." Casey crossed the room to the map and found their general location. The moon had tucked itself behind clouds, making it more difficult to see in the room. She didn't want to risk lighting a candle with the expansive windows in front visible from the street below.

"Huckabee strikes me as an orderly sort." Quinn joined her at the map and leaned close enough to see some of the detail. "Do you see these markings here?"

"I'm not an owl. I can barely see the outlines."

He cast a curious glance at her. "Owl?"

"They have keen night vision."

Amusement tinged his voice when he asked, "How do you know owls see well at night?"

"My sister, Rose. She's a wealth of random information. What were you trying to show me?"

"Yes, but an owl? Why not a raccoon or a toad?"

She ignored him and continued to search on her own.

"I didn't ask before, but I find now I must." Quinn tugged at the edge of her black duster, similar to his own. "Do you have an ensemble for every occasion?"

Casey swiped at his hand and ignored his soft laugh. She tapped a finger against the map. "What do you see that I don't?"

Quinn placed a hand on each of her arms and scooted her a foot to the left where he had been standing. He released her and tapped five points on the map between Durango and Silverton. "If you look carefully, you can see these dots are darker than the surrounding lines and marks. They may not be significant. However—"

"Everything is important until we rule it out as immaterial." Casey was reminded about the alleged witness. Would Johnson risk his career by helping Huckabee to cover up a crime? And what did either have to gain? "How did you know I would come here tonight?"

The abrupt change in subject gave Quinn a moment's pause. "Between the intrusion into your room and discovering your new accommodation was next to mine, I did not think you'd be up for sleeping."

Annoyed at his accuracy, she pressed on. "Fine, but how did you know I would be here?"

Quinn shrugged. "It's what I would do." He took a pencil and clean sheet of paper from a table and returned to the map. His face was mere inches away as he made a rough copy of the dots' placement. When he finished, he saw Casey with hands on her hips, and though he couldn't clearly see her expression, he somehow knew she glared at him. He spoke through a smile when he told her, "We are not as different as you might wish us to be."

CHAPTER 14

"We're not as alike as you want to believe." Casey stilled and took advantage of the sudden silence to listen. "Someone is here." She nudged him back into the office, and once inside, Quinn quietly replaced the bar across the door.

The sound of footsteps rose through the floorboards. Neither moved, spoke, and barely breathed as the steps stopped and movement along the wall with the hidden stairs indicated they were about to have company.

Quinn took a single, long stride until he stood next to Casey on the carpet. There was only one place to hide, but going back into the other room would leave the bar out of place. Casey didn't particularly care if they were found, for they had her convoluted agreement from Huckabee, but she had to consider it might not be Ellison Huckabee downstairs. He didn't seem the type to work in the middle of the night, not with a wife at home or a mistress to warm his bed.

The door to the stairway was still open, and so far, it

remained as dark as when they walked through it earlier. Quinn tapped her on the shoulder, and when she looked up at him, he pointed to the desk. Casey shook her head at his obvious idea for her to crawl underneath. He indicated the desk again, and she once more denied him.

In a surprising move, Quinn covered her mouth with his hand, lifted her up and against him, and carried her into the dark stairway. He did not put her down until he pressed her to the far wall, with Quinn blocking anyone or anything that might come into the portal.

Casey hadn't realized the depth of the landing. For spite's sake, she wanted to stomp on his foot and push him aside, but a soft creak from downstairs kept her silent and immobile. Quinn closed the door to the office without making much sound. His warm breath ruffled strands of the ebony wig she wore to cover her dark, copper locks. Of their own volition, her hands held onto the edges of Quinn's duster, and either he didn't mind or he failed to notice.

Light filtered into the portal from Ellison's office, yet no one ascended the stairs. Sweat trickled down Casey's back, but she remained as still as Quinn. She didn't know how he made no sound while still breathing, and she might have worried if she couldn't feel the rise and fall of his chest.

What seemed an interminably long time ended up being less than a minute by the count Casey made of the seconds as they passed. When the doorway closed, Quinn eased his upper body back a little, but his feet remained in the same place. Minutes later, when the footsteps retreated and the door to Ellison's office closed, Quinn stepped away.

"Are you all right?"

She nodded, even though he couldn't see her. Then again, perhaps he could with his owl-like eyes. Casey managed a smile, if only for herself. "I'm fine. He left through the back door."

"What?"

"Whoever was just here left through the back door."

"The door with the picked lock."

Casey nodded again and stepped around him. "Which means it wasn't Ellison. I'm certain he would have called for the marshal." She needed fresh, night air free of dust and the distracting scent of male. Confident they were now alone, Casey made her way down the stairs and through the hall to the back door. She inched it open and waited. The area behind the building sounded deserted, and she pushed the door open far enough to slip outside.

The mountain air filled her lungs, and she leaned her head back and allowed herself a few seconds to enjoy the spattering of stars light up the sky. When she heard Quinn behind her, she withdrew the picks from her pocket and worked the keyhole until the door was once again locked.

"Where did you learn to do that?"

"Practice. You can't pick a lock?"

"Clumsily, but yes. Relocking is another matter."

Casey didn't offer a response when she stuffed the picks back in her coat pocket and scratched at the edges of her scalp. She had wanted to be away from the room next to Quinn's earlier, but now she could think of nothing better than stripping down, loosening her hair, and wiping away the grime and sweat from her skin.

"It will be better if no one sees us returning together."

"What, you haven't stowed away a change of clothes somewhere close like last time?"

Casey had, but she would not confess to him. She made sure no one ever saw the real her going into the same place while in disguise. "We can talk after I've slept a few hours." She didn't get far before Quinn's fingers grasped her arm. "I'm tired, Quinn."

He held out a hand. "Fine. Give me back the drawing."

She fumbled in her pocket for the drawing she swiped from Quinn while on the landing and handed it to him. "How did you know?"

"I notice everything about you, Cassandra." Quinn grinned and unfolded the paper. "Now, we can go back to your room and give this a careful study, or . . ."

"Or?"

"I was hoping you'd accept the first offer."

"You're an infuriating man."

"What's one more shortcoming added to the ever-growing list you've already started?" He waved the drawing in front of her. "Well?"

"Wait here." Casey checked again to make sure no one was around before darting deeper into the darkness. She sneaked into the rickety shed where she stashed her valise this time and made quick work of changing. An audible sigh escaped her lips when she removed the ebony wig and gingerly massaged her scalp. Her fingers moved deftly through the strands of hair as she braided, then twisted her hair and pinned it up.

The clothing proved more difficult with no light, and the quick rap on the door told her she'd taken longer than planned. Casey remained quiet on the chance it was not Quinn standing on the other side.

"Casey?"

"Almost done." She tucked her shirt, secured her skirt, and hoped she looked presentable enough to walk up to her room. She stuffed the other clothes into the valise and opened the shed door and let in the moonlight no longer hidden behind clouds.

Quinn peered inside. "I do not think even a harlot would go in there." He stood close enough to give her appearance a leisurely study. On impulse, he tucked a loose curl behind her ear. "Definitely the back door for you."

"Really?"

He smiled and held out an arm. "Just an old married couple on an evening walk."

Casey accepted his arm and together they returned to the hotel and avoided any other patrons. Given the late hour, Casey was surprised to see anyone about, but behind the polished front desk, a bored clerk ignored them as they walked up the stairs.

Minutes later, they were inside her room, but Quinn stopped by the door and bent down to pick up an envelope. "Who knows you're here? It says M. Pennyworth."

Casey held out a hand and then read the return address. "It's my sister."

"I thought Mrs. Pennyworth manages your sister's house."

"She does. Rose enjoys intrigue."

"How did the desk clerk know to leave this here?"

"I used Pennyworth to register the room."

She couldn't decipher the half-smile blended with the look that said he still had questions simmering beneath the surface.

He backed out of the room and said as he was closing the door, "I'll return soon."

Grateful for a few minutes of privacy and realizing Quinn had left for that purpose, Casey placed the sealed letter on the bed near the pillow, then cleaned herself up the best she could at the water basin and changed into a clean skirt and shirt. She folded the others and set them aside to be taken to the laundry later.

True to his word, Quinn reappeared a short while later. He had also cleaned up, though he still wore the same clothes and now carried a small field notebook and pencil. He moved the small table next to the bed along with the only chair. "This will be easiest, I think." Quinn stood next to the chair, which left the bed for Casey. Once she sat, he spread the drawing out for them to review. Casey unrolled a map of Colorado next to the drawing.

At Quinn's raised brow, she said, "I bought it from the land office on the day we arrived." Casey ran her finger over the rail line Quinn drew to connect the points. "How sure are you of the accuracy of the dots?"

"Sure enough." He placed the drawing on the map and lined up the dots and rail line to the same area between Durango and Silverton. "Five markings on the map, each one within a few miles of a town."

"This one here." Casey pressed a finger to the marking closest to one of the two towns.

"Hermosa?"

Casey nodded but remained silent.

"Casey?"

She flicked her hand in his direction. "Quiet." She stood and paced the room, reaching into her memory bank for the elusive file. "1896? No, not that long ago." When she reached one end of the room, Casey pivoted and walked to the other, repeating the pattern and ignoring all else around her. "1897? Peterson's case. No, Sampson's. Got it!"

She returned to the table and looked at Quinn rather than the map. "Hermosa came up in an investigation in 1897, it was May or June. Another agent was working a forgery case, and Hermosa was one of a dozen places they thought the forgers might be hiding."

"Casey, there are all kinds of places in these mountains for people to hide, so it's not an unreasonable assumption. What makes this recollection worth mentioning?"

"Let me finish." Casey grabbed his pencil from between the pages of his notebook and wrote the other names she remembered. "There were a lot more, but three of the towns were in Colorado. Creede and Leadville were the other two."

"All heavy mining areas."

"Exactly."

"What about the other places on the list, of those you can remember?"

Casey studied the list carefully. She had not been to all of them but knew enough about the surrounding territories and states to say with some accuracy, "Not mining. I was sure—"

"You might still be." Quinn took his pencil back and circled two of the towns on the list. "This Kansas town is in an area known for oil drilling. And this one in Utah . . . I had a client there—"

"As a lawyer or bounty hunter?"

"Lawyer, and I fired him, but never mind. The client was a wealthy banker, though not the only one in the area."

Casey considered the new information. "If we proceed on the assumption that the 1897 forgery case is connected to our case, then this case is likely also about forgeries."

"Correct, except . . ."

"Yes?"

"You said forgeries. Any murders in any of those previous cases? Did they ever catch anyone?"

"No murders and no arrest to my knowledge." Casey had been visiting her uncle in Chicago at the time, which is how she had heard about it. "I have someone I can ask if they know anything more, and he'll keep it to himself if I ask him."

"A beau?"

Casey bit the inside of her cheek to keep from smiling. "He is the dearest man I know. He is also my uncle and the reason I am a Pinkerton." She studied the section on the map between Durango and Silverton. "Hermosa might make sense, but these others don't. As far as I know, there aren't any towns near these three markings." She glanced at him. "You are certain about their placement?"

"Yes."

"All right then. There is a social this week here at the hotel. Ellison Huckabee himself is the host. Apparently, he rents out the main common rooms once a year and puts on a grand affair for everyone he deems important." Casey rolled up the Colorado map and set it out of the way on the dresser.

"It is amazing what you accomplished during the brief times we have been apart. How did you manage an invitation?"

Casey didn't try to hide her cheeky grin this time. "Cassandra McKenzie did not. Cassandra and Quinn Morgan of the Philadelphia Morgans did."

"Philadelphia?"

"My birthplace, and where my mother's family still lives. Subterfuge is more effective when truth is at the core."

"Yes, but does it ever exhaust you, pretending to be different people?"

Casey eyed the letter sitting by her pillow and thought of her sister and uncle, both of whom possessed the same zeal for solving puzzles as she did. Then she thought of her mother, with whom she had nothing in common, and who had once asked her something eerily similar. "Haven't you ever wanted to be someone else? To see if people treat you differently?"

Sensing a more serious tone in the conversation now, Quinn watched her and slowly shook his head. "As a lawyer, people have to know who I am to trust me. As a bounty hunter, they only have to know I can get the job done."

"Interesting."

Quinn returned the table to its place by the window. "You enjoy it, don't you?"

"I do. The people who matter know who I am. Everyone else doesn't matter enough for me to care what they think."

"What's that?"

She took Quinn's abrupt change in subject to mean he didn't have an opinion on her last statement. "What is what?"

Quinn knelt and picked up a half-sheet-sized paper folded once. "This."

"Oh!" Casey snatched it from him. "I forgot." She patted the sides of her skirt and glanced at the stack of clothes she'd changed out of earlier. Had she put it in her coat? "Never mind. I took it from the office."

He grabbed it back and unfolded it. "When?"

"When we were in there?"

"Granted, I knew you took the drawing because I felt it, but this penchant you have for stealing—"

"Borrowing."

"Stealing will get you into trouble one day." Quinn perused the paper, his brow furrowing as he read it a second time. "This is a lot of shares."

"That's what I originally thought, and it was just sitting there. No one misplaces such a valuable document unless they're incompetent, or it is—"

"Not real."

"You were going to work on your annoying habit of finishing my sentences."

"I'll start tomorrow." He motioned her closer. "If this is a forgery, then it's superb work. I've handled enough of these to know the real thing apart from a fake."

"And this one looks real?"

"At first glance. However, lawyers, agents, and governments, etc. can use different methods of hiding little things in their documents that are used for verification. We'll need to get an authentic certificate from the company's office for comparison and speak with whoever issues the documents for Huckabee Mining."

"Pitt & Tate Mining was a small outfit out of Silverton."

"Was?"

"Yes. They went bankrupt last year. One witness in the original forgery case worked for them. Otherwise, I know nothing about them."

"Did they go bankrupt because of the investigation?"

Casey shook her head. "They struggled for years, so it's unrelated, which is what makes this certificate suspect. For a company like Huckabee Mining, this would be worth a lot of money. For a defunct outfit like Pitt & Tate, it's worthless, so why keep it? And why would it be in Huckabee's office?"

Her smile widened and her eyes gleamed. "You realize this brings us closer to the possibility that the open Pinkerton case from 1897 is linked to this one. If it's not the same people—and the murder suggests it might not be—then it is someone close to them. The similarities are too coincidental."

Quinn withdrew his pocket watch and noted the time. "I agree, and we can continue this on the journey tomorrow."

"Excuse me?"

"Tomorrow. We'll ride—"

"I don't think so."

"We could take the train, but they will not stop where we want simply because we ask them to, Casey." Quinn started for the door.

"I don't ride."

He looked as though he didn't quite believe her. "Ever?"

"It's a long story, but I think the train will be better."

"The train would be faster but not better. Besides, we will have to take the train partway to save some time." Quinn patted her on the shoulder. "You'll do fine. I brought my horse with me, so we'll rent you one from the stockyard tomorrow." Without another word, Quinn left the room, leaving Casey to stare after him.

CHAPTER 15

There are worse ways to die.

Those words flickered through Casey's mind as she sat atop a pretty quarter horse. Its rich, golden coat and mane and tail of white, with a few dark strands blended in, suited the sprightly mare. Her personality had won Casey over in the stockyard, and while she still thought her the prettiest horse she'd ever seen, Casey expected to be tossed over her head at any moment.

"How are you doing back there?"

The long valley spread far in two directions, flanked by rolling mountains covered in rich, green pine and aspens in shades of pale yellow and dark gold. The sun granted them with its glorious presence from the moment they boarded the train in Durango. Crisp air filled her lungs, and for a few moments, as she sat atop the horse, Casey thought herself in paradise.

What a shame it would be to mar such beauty with Quinn's dead body.

"Casey?"

"I heard you," she mumbled.

He slowed his horse until hers was abreast of them. "You're not still vexed, are you? I thought you liked the mare. I'm told she's a new purchase from, and I quote, 'a citified gent who didn't make it out of his first saloon fight.'"

"*Her* I like just fine."

"How does someone in your line of work not ride?"

"The advent of trains has made it possible for me to enjoy them while both my feet are on the ground." Casey adjusted her seat and veered the mare a few inches to the right to avoid a sharp-edged rock.

"You know how to ride."

"I never said I couldn't." Casey pulled gently on the reins to stop the horse and held out a hand. "Let me see your map again."

"You studied it for twenty minutes on the train." Quinn handed it over. "We're going in the right direction."

"You hope we are. Unless cartographer is part of your vast resume, I intend to remain skeptical." Casey consulted the watch she'd pinned to her vest that morning and looked back at the map. "We got off the train in Hermosa—"

"Clever how you got the conductor to take the time for us to disembark there."

"Railroads like the Pinkertons. Now, we have ridden approximately one mile south, and according to your map, we should be close to the first mysterious marking." She folded the small map and handed it back to him. "There aren't any known mines around here. You convinced them to add a stock car for the horses. Curious how that was arranged before I knew there would be horses."

She encouraged the mare back into a steady walk and studied the terrain and mountainsides for signs of caves, burrows, drills, or anything else that could indicate a mining operation.

"*Known* mines is the key," Quinn said. "We're looking for unknown. I thought you liked puzzles."

"I do. I also like to solve cases, and even though . . ."

Quinn drew his gelding alongside the mare. "What do you see?"

"Look at the tall pine directly in front of you, then follow the tree line to the left. Does that look like a shadow to you or—"

"A cave."

Casey's leg muscles burned from the short time spent in the saddle, and she swore when this case ended, she would never ride a horse again. But the case wasn't anywhere close to over, so with heels down and legs straight she squeezed inward with her calves to get the horse moving again. Another light use of pressure and the mare shifted into a gentle canter, then a gallop. Casey held on tight and tried to remember the long-ago lessons about balance, but after a few minutes, instinct took over and she enjoyed the ride.

Quinn's gelding advanced and gained on her mare, which turned out to be fortuitous since Casey's memory seemed to be momentarily devoid of any knowledge on how to stop.

"You'll have to explain to me sometime your aversion to horses."

It took Casey a few seconds to catch her breath enough before she could respond. Quinn did not appear to have the same difficulty. "Solve the case before me, and I will answer any single question you want."

He didn't smile, but it was close. "And what boon do you get if you solve the case first?"

"The same. Any question."

"Agreed." Quinn got down and walked around the front of his horse to help her off the mare. She slid easily into his arms but let go too soon and her feet landed with a jarring thud on the ground. "We'll work on the dismount." He chuckled and handed her the reins.

She'd wait until they were in the cave. No one would find him there, at least not before the critters got to him.

"Casey?"

She shook away thoughts of her murderous plot. "There appears to be an outcropping up there where we can hide the horses." Without waiting for Quinn, Casey hiked the slope. Once there, she assessed the options and walked a dozen more yards to a grouping of boulders planted in another hillside and large enough to offer cover. A massive oak extended far enough over the giant rocks to offer shade.

"They should be good here long enough for us to look

inside." Quinn checked the surrounding ground for holes and finding none, selected a sturdy branch a few inches above his head.

"Aren't you worried your horse will get away?"

Quinn peered at the knot Casey made of the mare's reins and shook his head. Once he secured his horse, he saw to the mare. "Tie her up too tight and too close to Raider and she'll hurt herself or him if she's spooked." He fixed the mess and wrapped the reins loosely and twice around another sturdy branch a few extra feet away. "Better they be able to get away if something is wrong than injure themselves trying to escape. I'd rather we lose our horses than they lose their lives."

Casey agreed. "Seems I have much to learn."

"How did you learn to ride without knowing the rest?"

"We had a man who cared for the horses, and they were always saddled before we reached the stables." Embarrassment crept into her voice, though there was no basis for it. Good fortune had followed her from birth, and many things she learned to do later in life were thanks to a variety of inadvertent teachers who would not do for her what she could do for herself. She was proud of her accomplishments and skills earned over the years, and thanks to her uncle, Casey wielded both gun and blade with equal proficiency. His only regret, he once confessed, was not getting her back up on a horse.

She walked back down the slope and to the cave before Quinn could press her further. Casey stared at the cavernous mouth and momentarily rethought her next move. "If there is a bear, I have a gun." She nodded once to herself, straightened her shoulders, and walked a few feet. Her right boot connected with an object, causing it to topple and clatter. Casey bent down, and by the meager light seeping in from the entrance, she picked up the fallen lamp.

"Do you always have to do everything alone?" Quinn asked as she returned to the light.

"Habit."

"Handy finding the lamp, but . . . what have you done to yourself?"

Casey had noticed no pain until Quinn took the lamp from her grasp and placed it on the ground. Blood seeped from beneath her leather glove down her wrist. A thin cut on her left palm revealed itself when he gingerly removed the glove and stuffed it in his duster pocket. "It is barely a scratch."

"Could have fooled me. We need to stop the bleeding."

She did not want to agree, but blood continued to drizzle down her arm and stain the sleeve of her shirt despite the pressure Quinn put on it. "Petticoat."

"What?"

"There is enough of it to make a bandage."

Quinn raised a brow but said nothing as he produced a thin blade of his own. Careful not to look anywhere he shouldn't, he lifted the edge of her skirt and sliced through a strip of the white, cotton petticoat. "It needs to be cleaned first."

"I will clean it later." Casey tried to keep the edge of pain from her voice. The slice to her skin now throbbed just below the surface.

Quinn pressed one end of the fabric against her wound and wrapped the remaining strip around her hand four times before tying it off at the wrist. "Too tight?"

Casey shook her head and flexed her hand, then spread her fingers wide. "It is already feeling better." She flexed again. "Thank you." She picked up the lantern Quinn set down earlier. "It appears to have been broken before now. There is enough oil in here to last long enough for us to see what else is inside."

Before she could dig out a match from her duster pocket, Quinn produced one.

"I noticed the knife sheathed in your boot." He put the matches back in a pocket. "What else do you have hidden down there?"

Casey ignored his question as the wick flamed. "Ready?"

Quinn stopped her before she entered the cave before him. "You have already proven yourself immensely capable of many tasks and without my assistance could no doubt take down whole criminal networks on your own." He pressed a hand to his chest then gestured to the opening. "Allow me to play the gentleman."

A light, pink blush colored Casey's cheeks. She passed him the lantern and stepped out of the way. For her part, she held back the smaller branches of a wild raspberry bush and waited until he entered first. Quinn ducked his head a few inches to pass through the mouth.

"Do you smell that?"

Casey did not have to breathe in for the chemical smell to fill her senses. "It smells like one of Rose's exploding experiments."

She saw the questioning look on Quinn's face. "Never mind. Dry rock and some kind of chemical. No mine is registered here, so how did they keep it secret? And if all five markings on the map at Huckabee mining correspond to a hidden mine, then they have to be long played out." They walked a few dozen feet when she felt her boot slip a little and balanced her body to prevent a fall.

"All right?"

"Yes. I am smelling water now, and the ground is damp."

"I smell it, too, and hear it. Must be the river." Quinn stopped and held out an arm until she reached him. "Over there, to the right." He held the lantern in the same direction.

"This is unexpected."

"But answers a lot of questions. Do you have more than a blade in your boot?"

Casey patted the Colt holstered against her hip. "Yes. You?"

Quinn nodded. "As much as I want to find out what is in those bags, their presence means someone will return soon."

"We need to see what's inside, Quinn." Casey walked carefully in the dim light and crouched next to one of the large burlap sacks.

"Whatever is in there—"

"I have a job to do, but you don't need to be here." The sharp edge of her knife sliced through the twine holding the top of the sack closed. "This is not Huckabee's missing money."

Quinn moved closer and hovered the light over their discovery. "No, but still quite valuable. I recognize some of the equipment." He handed her the lantern, took her knife, and opened a second bag. "And these."

Casey leaned toward him and peered inside. "Engraving plates. You were right. We need to get out of here, but we are taking these with us."

"The horses can't carry all of this."

She tried to heft a bag over her shoulder and failed the first time. "No, but we can hide it somewhere else. These have to be destroyed. We can bury them. The railroad keeps a small cache of dynamite locked up near the water station in Hermosa. We won't need much to blow up the entrance, and it will give me enough time to—"

"No."

"I have accepted you on this case, and even welcomed it, but you do not get to tell me no this time. My superiors must be informed, and they need to notify the Secret Service. Even with my limited counterfeiting experience, I recognize the tools of an advanced operation."

"We can discuss this at length once we're breathing fresh air."

Casey remained still and unfocused on him.

"Did you hear me?"

"Quiet," she said in a harsh whisper. In a fluid swipe, she took the lantern and blew out the flame. "Listen."

They kept silent and immobile, and within less than a minute, the sound of scraping and muffled voices carried toward them.

"This isn't a mine shaft, Casey, which means there probably isn't another way out."

She pushed her duster out of the way in case she had to reach for her Colt. "Then we go forward."

CHAPTER 16

The voices grew louder and then stopped. Casey could not make out what the two men were saying—and she was certain two of them had entered the cave. She often found herself in unexpected places, with few options for escape until an imperfect opportunity presented itself. And yet, she was usually alone, with no one else to think or worry about.

Quinn could take care of himself, and she did not think he would appreciate her concern over his welfare, but she could not crush the uneasiness that something might happen to him.

His arm snaked around her waist—she must speak to him about the liberties he made a habit of taking with her—and shifted her until she faced the deeper, darker part of the cave they had yet to walk.

He leaned close, his warm breath tickling the skin on her neck, and whispered, "Look forward. The light."

Casey preferred to shoot her way out of the cave than do what he suggested. She shook her head and reached for her Colt.

"There could be more of them outside. We will not risk our

lives unless we have to." Quinn released the hold he had on her shooting hand and quietly led her toward the faint light.

Casey knew what light meant and hoped she was wrong. She couldn't deny there might be more men waiting outside, and she agreed that no justification existed to defend the needless risk of life. She would have risked it, though, when faced alone with the alternative.

Water traveled through the ground somewhere nearby and echoed against the stone and dirt walls around them. It provided the cover they needed to walk without alerting the other men. The light grew brighter the farther they walked, until the cave curved and opened into a small—too small—tunnel.

Her chest tightened, and she held a fist against it, pounding once, then twice, to release the breath that refused to come out.

"Casey?"

She could see him somewhat in the dull light. He rubbed a strong hand over her back in slow motions, directly over her lungs, and held her face still, forcing her to look at him. How did he know to do that? She planned to ask him if they made it out alive. When Casey thought she might suffocate, the pressure on her chest loosened by degrees until she could exhale a deep breath.

"Why didn't you say something?"

It had been a long time since Casey had been in a situation where she experienced such fear over something so mundane as an enclosed space. She avoided such places for good reason and would have been all right knowing the way out until Quinn revealed her weakness. Claustrophobia, someone had called, but Casey did not believe any phobia applied to her.

Control mattered in her line of work, and she would not relinquish it now. "I will be all right." They heard shouting, which likely meant the men had discovered their cache disturbed. "Go."

Instead of going into the tunnel first, Quinn helped her forward. "The light isn't too far down, which means it will be quick. There looks to be plenty of room for us both if we move along close to the ground." He held her chin between his fingers. "Are you sure?"

With surprise no longer on their side, shooting their way through was no longer an option. In answer to his question, Casey got down on all fours and crawled into the tunnel. Every few seconds, Quinn touched her leg or boot, offering her comfort in his nearness.

The shaft proved longer than expected, and the uncomfortable tightness inched its way back into Casey's chest. She started humming in her mind, an old Scottish tune she remembered her father singing to her when she was a child. The name of the song escaped her, but it brought enough comfort to get her through the last dozen feet of the tunnel and into the light.

She clambered to her feet and sucked in fresh, dry air. Quinn did not give her time to enjoy it, though. He grasped her hand

and ran with her to where they left the horses. Without a word, he half-tossed her into the mare's saddle before she could lift herself into it and swung onto the back of Raider.

He did not ask again if she was all right. They guided their horses with as much speed and safety as they could over the rocks and through the brush until the land opened enough for them to gallop, and run they did with the firing of bullets behind them. Quinn had been right in his suspicions, for the gunfire came from more than two guns, which means more men had been outside after all.

What had they stumbled into? How far and wide did the ring of thieves and conspiracy stretch? Determined to live long enough to get her answers, Casey concentrated on staying in the saddle. Half a mile later, they came to a stop, the horses breathing as heavily as their riders. "They will not stop, and the train won't pass through Hermosa for hours yet."

Quinn took in their surroundings before pulling out his map.

"You won't need the map. There is a ranch a mile or so south." She gulped in another deep breath and felt her heart slow its tempo.

"How big?"

"Large, I think. I overheard a wrangler the other night in the saloon mention it."

"Rock Creek Ranch by chance?"

"Sounds right. How did you know?"

Quinn put the map away. "From the map in Huckabee's

office."

"We can't risk it, then." Casey considered their meager options. "Either Ellison Huckabee is aware of the locations on his map, or someone in his office is involved. Huckabee is pompous enough not to want to risk his reputation, so my wager is on the latter."

"You might be right, but now we have to find shelter close to Hermosa until the train comes through."

Casey smoothed her uninjured hand over the mare's neck. "Turns out getting back in the saddle wasn't as difficult as I thought it would be. Let's keep riding. We have enough of a start on them." She appreciated he did not ask again if she was sure. It had been difficult enough for her to have shown weakness back in the cave. Casey wouldn't let it happen again.

TWO HOURS LATER, they rode into Durango, dusty, thirsty, and in desperate need of baths. They walked when their horses needed it, and ran in between, alternating between both, hoping to keep enough distance between them and the men from the cave. Casey knew the men had not gotten a good look at more than their backs, since they'd been closer to the mouth of the cave. Once out of the rougher riding clothes, it would be almost impossible for those men to find Casey and Quinn in town. The horses, however, were going to be harder to hide if the men got a good look during the pursuit. His chestnut gelding was fine, but not too out of the ordinary. Casey's pretty Palomino, on the other hand, was distinctive enough to remember.

Once at the stockyard, Quinn dismounted first and hurried to Casey's side. She accepted his help without comment. Her back and legs ached as they never had before, and while riding would not be an issue again, she still preferred her own two feet or the convenience of a comfortable rail car.

"What happened to you two?" Mr. Adams appeared in the massive entry to the stable. He glanced up at the sky almost as if wondering how he might have missed the storm that explained their appearance.

"Snake spooked the horses."

"That'll do it." The stockyard manager held the reins of both animals, but he focused on Casey. "I know you from somewhere, Mrs. Morgan?"

"We rented the carriage, Mr. Adams."

"Nah, well, maybe." He shrugged. "It'll come to me. I don't forget faces, even though lots of folks come through Durango."

Casey kept her exhaled breath of relief silent. No one had ever come close to recognizing her as anyone other than who she portrayed to them, and it had been years since she had been in the area. "Is the mare for sale?"

It was unclear which of the men were more surprised. Mr. Adams looked first to Quinn, who offered him no direction. "She's a fine piece of horseflesh."

"She is, which is why I would like to buy her." Casey offered him a smile that flirted on the line between coy and friendly. It was a look she reserved for whenever she wanted something to go her way, without giving the wrong impression.

"Well, seeing as how Mr. Morgan has been so generous, I reckon two hundred dollars."

It worked every time. Casey smiled. A good saddle horse could set a person back upwards of three hundred dollars, so she considered the man's price a fair one. He was right about the mare—a fine piece of horseflesh indeed. Not one to spend money idly, she stunned herself at the immediate agreement on price and her eagerness to buy a horse.

What was she going to do with a horse when she rode the train almost everywhere? She chose to worry about the details later. "I accept. Please see she is groomed and looked after."

Quinn, wearing a smile of amusement, handed the stockyard manager enough banknotes to cover the purchase and more to cover the mare's boarding and feed for another week. The glance he sent in Casey's direction silenced her forthcoming objection. "Thank you, Mr. Adams. I need to see my wife back to the hotel now."

With a newfound fortune in his hands, Mr. Adams smiled wide, tipped his hat at them both, and yelled out for his young assistant.

"It is clear, Cassandra McKenzie, that you do not know how to horse trade."

She slipped her arm into his—for appearance's sake, she told herself—and they made their way to the hotel. "She was worth the price."

"I agree, but judging by how big his eyes got when I handed him the money, he likely paid only half that price for her."

"Perhaps, but I wanted her."

Those simple words, spoken with a careless determination Quinn admired, revealed one more layer of Cassandra McKenzie, and still, he wanted much more. "Fair enough."

"I will pay you back."

"No need."

She stopped them both near the hotel entrance and stared up at his face for several seconds.

"All right, you'll pay me back."

He whisked her inside; neither acknowledged the desk clerk. It was mid-afternoon, after lunch and long enough ahead of dinner, so they were able to avoid running into anyone who might recognize them or wonder at their condition. Quinn left her at the room, and before he could walk back to his, she grabbed his sleeve to pull him back. Casey unlocked her room and dragged him inside.

"Quit your grinning, Quinn Morgan. This is not a display of flirtation or an invitation for any—"

"Shenanigans?"

She released him and shook her head. "How is it no matter how many years a man has been on this earth, he never loses the child in him that finds humor at the oddest times?"

"Probably something we're born with. It helps the male species survive."

Casey laughed, but not so loud he could hear. When she returned to his side, she handed him money. "You paid too much for boarding."

"I know." Quinn didn't accept the stack of banknotes. "Why is this important to you? Could be it's a gift, which would make this gesture rather churlish on your part."

"An extravagant gift." She held the money out closer to him. "It would be ungrateful of me, so what if I told you buying her is something I need to do for myself?"

Quinn studied her face for several seconds before nodding once. He took the banknotes and folded them into his vest pocket.

"It is a wonder thieves have not set upon either of us." Casey thought again of the generous bathtub in the Denver house. She could use some of those wonderful, scented salts Mrs. Pennyworth always kept stocked. The copper tub Miss Mashburn left in her room would have to suffice, and it would be a while before enough boiling water could be brought up for it.

"Cassandra?"

She shook away her musings. "Cassandra now? And here I thought you preferred Casey."

"I like them both, and I said your name twice. You went away again." He lightly tapped the side of her head. "What we went through out there, in the cave and shaft."

"I have been through worse."

Quinn suspected as much. Her recovery from their ordeal was not a typical woman's reaction, at least not any woman he had ever met. "We have a lot of work left to do."

Contacting Mr. Johnson and the Secret Service was at the top of her list of what came next. No, they could wait long enough for her to wash off the caked dirt and sweat. With her mind set, she ushered Quinn from her room. "Give me an hour."

"An hour won't give us much time before the soiree you finagled invitations to this evening."

How could she have forgotten? Casey thought out what they could accomplish before the party and decided there was still enough time. "One hour."

CHAPTER 17

Quinn consulted his watch for the second time and checked the round clock on the wall behind the bar to make sure his was not out of step. He returned to the base of the staircase again but did not stop there. In less than a minute, he stood outside her room and knocked.

She opened the door, grumbling about impatient men, and motioned him inside to wait. "I am three minutes late."

"Five." Quinn no longer cared. She could spend another hour doing whatever females do to prepare themselves for an evening, and he would happily wait. He believed himself long ago immune to the obvious flirtations and efforts of a beautiful woman, but Cassandra McKenzie was not obvious, at least not on purpose. When he had first glimpsed her at the restaurant in Colorado Springs, he experienced some attraction, yet curiosity proved more powerful and grew with each encounter.

Quinn had no words for the gut-tugging interest now overwhelming both his mind and body.

He rarely gave much thought to women's fashion, again, until he'd met her. She selected each ensemble to suit a specific purpose, but none achieved their goal so much as the gown she wore now. The green silk and velvet gown edged with dark fur skimmed and flowed from her shoulders to the carpet. It tucked in at all the right places and hung loosely in others just enough to make a man wonder what the material covered. Cut at a slight curve across her chest, she revealed nothing, and yet no woman before her could ever claim—

"Quinn?"

"Yes?"

"Did you even hear me?"

He thought of the bottle of Glenturret a grateful client gave him three years prior. It still sat three-quarters full on a shelf in the house he occasionally visited in Denver. Quinn considered fine whiskey a drink for celebration—until now. Two fingers of the amber liquid would suit him nicely, but he'd settle for water at the party. He preferred to keep his wits, which was a little challenging at the moment. "No, I did not. I don't recall that dress being with the others when your room was tossed."

Casey—no, tonight she looked like a Cassandra—tilted her head a fraction to the left as she often did when studying him.

"I keep it wrapped in tissue." She smoothed her hands over the fine silk. "Is it too much? This is the only evening dress I travel with since it doesn't take up too much room. My mother selected it, and no matter how rustic our location, those people down there are more her kind than mine."

Quinn silently thanked whatever master created the dress to fit her perfectly, and another note of gratitude went out to her mother, for having the wisdom to choose it. He noticed before she did not wear bustles and she did not wear one now. Quinn appreciated a practical woman.

She picked up a thick, black shawl and draped it so the fabric caught enticingly at her lower back, and the edges hung one over each elbow. The long, loose sleeves in the same green silk swayed a little as she walked toward him.

"You look the part of a city gentleman's wife." She stopped in front of him and he lifted her hands in his. "You're beautiful."

He took advantage of her momentary loss of words to fold her arm through his and escort her from the room. Moving past any potential awkwardness, he said, "Huckabee is downstairs, and I recognized a few of the clerks from his office, but most of the attendees appear to be from out of town. Or, if they are from here, I haven't seen them since our arrival."

"As I said, more my mother's people."

"Is she one for parties?"

Casey shook her head, then stopped halfway and nodded. "Sometimes. She keeps busy, though with what I could not tell you."

"Do you take more after her or your father?"

"Beautiful?"

The question in her voice took him back to what he let slip in her room. Was it a slip of words, he wondered, or did he enjoy surprising her? Both, he concluded, and kept it to himself. They paused at the top of the stairs.

"Do you mind that I said it?"

"No, I just . . . no, I don't mind. I hope you still think so after we return."

Quinn groaned. "From where?"

"There is no need to think the worst. You will see, but we should make an appearance downstairs first, so we aren't missed later."

"Anyone who sees you in that dress is definitely going to miss you later."

Still, he followed her lead, interested in what she had in mind for later. She should be exhausted after their misadventure earlier. Instead, she walked with a light step and calm manner, which if he knew her better, he suspected might serve as a clue to what would happen next. He stopped then, halfway down the stairs, and forced her to do the same.

"You went out before you dressed for this evening."

It was not a question, and she did not attempt to obfuscate. "Yes." She lowered her voice to a whisper. "I told you I needed to send a telegram to Agent Johnson. I prefer to solve this case without interference, and we still don't know who we can trust, but the Secret Service needs to be informed. Besides, I had to wait for enough hot water to be brought up for a bath. I had plenty of time to dart out and send the telegram."

"Someone at the front desk would have delivered it."

She disagreed and tugged on his arm until he continued walking down the staircase. "Trust, remember. Why does it bother you?"

"What if one of the men from the cave were to recognize you?"

"They did not see enough of us as we rode past them."

Quinn swept a hand over the back of her hair and ended with a loose strand between his fingers. "How many women do you think have hair like this around here?"

She pushed his hand away. "I wore it in a braid under a hat. Stop worrying so much."

Disconcerted at her lack of worry for her own safety, Quinn let the matter drop for now and entered the gallery where many of the guests mingled. "There are more people here than I expected, which will make sneaking away easier." He glanced her way. "A hint would help."

Casey smiled sweetly at a nearby couple and barely moved her lips when she spoke. "Smile, Ellison Huckabee is coming this way."

Quinn did not smile, but he was cordial and accepted the offer when Huckabee held out his free hand. The other hand gripped a glass with more drink than could be good for the man. "I hope you two are enjoying yourselves." Huckabee's gaze lingered overly long during his inspection of Casey. Once finished, and in a conspiratorial voice, he said, "I had expected an update on your progress by now."

"It has only been a few days."

Huckabee acknowledged Quinn's comment briefly before turning to Casey. "No doubt you are aware of your reputation within your agency."

"No doubt." She leaned closer. "You will be pleased to hear you will have a report soon."

"Well, that is good news."

The surprise in Huckabee's voice did not lose footing before Quinn caught hold. He could not tell from Casey's expression if she also heard it.

"You have my promise." Casey accepted a drink from a passing waiter.

"Excellent." Huckabee turned at the sound of his name. "Ah, my wife." He motioned to Quinn and Casey. "Margaret, may I introduce you to business associates visiting from Denver. Mr. and Mrs. Morgan."

The lie came easily to Huckabee. Too easily for it not to have planned a story in case explanations were needed.

Mrs. Huckabee smiled, though Quinn noticed it did not reach her eyes. "A pleasure to meet you both. You are also in mining?"

"Mine acquisition," Quinn said smoothly. "We have yet to convince your husband that he should part with his."

"My Ellison is too sharp to sell a profitable venture." She then spoke to her husband too softly for anyone else to hear.

Huckabee patted his wife's hand and addressed them once more. "If you will both excuse me." He followed Mrs. Huckabee through the gallery and disappeared into the mass of partygoers.

"She's not a friendly sort. I don't think Mrs. Huckabee liked us."

"You."

"What?"

"The seething stare was not directed at me but you. If she is aware of her husband's past infidelity, then she probably doesn't like any woman who stands within a few feet of him. Don't take it personally."

"I won't. I haven't. It is strange, though."

"Mr. and Mrs. Morgan?" Mr. Linwood approached with three other men, each garbed as nattily as the next. "May I introduce Mr. Pritchard, our accountant, Mr. Nutting, our mine manager, and his son, Percy, who is an apprentice to Mr. Pritchard."

Mr. Nutting squeezed his son's shoulder. "He's going to be a fine accountant one day, and no better place to learn."

Quinn nodded to each of the men. "You are all to be commended for your fine work at Huckabee Mining."

"You're familiar with it, then?" Mr. Nutting asked.

"Only by reputation, which is why we are here. We labor under the hope that Huckabee will sell."

Surprise flashed across the faces of all four men. "He would never!" This came from Mr. Nutting, but it was evident the others agreed. Even Linwood did an admirable job of playing along with their ruse.

Casey smiled at each of them. "Do not worry, gentlemen. My husband failed to say Mr. Huckabee has adamantly refused the idea. Boundless optimism is his greatest flaw."

All four men laughed, some more forced than others. "You are indeed a fortunate woman if that is the worst of your husband's character."

Casey thanked Mr. Pritchard. "Mr. Huckabee has offered us the use of his wisdom and experience regarding his part of Colorado, so you will see more of us."

Mr. Linwood said, "The pleasure will be ours, Mrs. Morgan." It appeared only Quinn and Casey noticed the hesitation before he said her name. "Ah, there are the Bargers from St. Louis. Please excuse us, Mr. and Mrs. Morgan. Mr. Huckabee has tasked us with taking a turn through the crowd."

The men bowed their heads to Casey and said their goodbyes. Alone once again, Casey looped her arm through Quinn's. "I could use a walk to take in some fresh air."

"We are of a similar mind, my dear."

They said enough greetings on their way to give anyone who might wonder the impression of a relaxed and loving couple enjoying each other's company. Casey did not take even a sip from the glass and set it down on a table to be retrieved by a waiter.

Once outside, Casey draped the shawl over her shoulders and

tucked the edges into the top of her overskirt. Bits of rock and dirt shifted under their shoes as they walked in companionable silence. Quinn allowed her to keep the pace until they rounded the south corner of the hotel and walked toward the street on which Huckabee Mining Company's building stood.

"There are many who consider me an astute man, but damned if I can figure out what we're doing here."

Without warning, Casey steered him down a darker side street behind the building and picked up her pace. He remained silent only until she stopped at the back entrance of Huckabee's building.

"No."

"No what?"

"Whatever you're thinking, the answer is no."

Casey waited for someone to pass before whispering, "Badge and gun. I have both. Unless I'm mistaken about where you could keep a gun without me having felt it between the hotel and here, you have neither."

Quinn swept his gaze over her again, remembering every inch of the flowing skirts.

"I have them, and no, you can't see."

"Bigger and stronger puts me at an advantage."

They faced off in a ludicrous standstill neither could win if they wanted to remain incognito. She sighed and stood firm. "Trust me."

"I don't have to do anything, and did it occur to you that

trust is more easily earned when you aren't keeping secrets?"

"It is not a secret." She gave him her back, lifted her skirts to expose a leather pouch strapped to her leg, and stood straight, holding two of her lock-picking tools.

He yanked the tools from her grasp. "Give me a good reason."

She yanked the tools back. "If I'm right, then you will have your reason in a minute."

CHAPTER 18

Casey's hands, one tool in each, hovered near the lock. She bent forward and inspected it before testing the handle. It moved easily under her soft touch, and the door clicked open.

She entered, expecting Quinn to follow, which he did. However, the look he gave her once they were inside with the door closed behind them said more than he could with words.

"Well now, what 'ave we 'ere?"

A match flared and the wick of a small lantern burned to life. Casey wanted to smile—almost did—but she kept her face free from expression.

Quinn stepped between her and the two men in the passageway. "It seems, gentlemen, we have intruded."

"Right you did," the shorter of the two men said. His thick mustache moved at an odd angle when he spoke.

"We'll leave you to it." Quinn blocked Casey from their view and backed up two steps before turning.

"I don't think so." The taller man with streaks of gray in his hair and skin that had seen too much sun spoke this time. "What are you doin' 'ere?" He held a pistol at waist height and motioned for Quinn to move. "Let's see 'er."

"No."

Casey quickly rethought her strategy of keeping the plan to herself. She thought they would have more time. "What my husband means to say is we have business elsewhere."

"I saw you," the shorter one said. "Coming out of the Strater." He raised his own pistol and pointed it directly at Quinn's chest. Quinn did not flinch.

"We are guests of the hotel." Casey studied the face of each man and recognized the subtle twitches and movements as signs of impatience. "None of us obviously want our presence here to become known to the marshal. Might I suggest we each do what we came to do and leave quietly?"

The tall one looked at Quinn. "You let 'er speak for you?"

Quinn's expression remained impassive. "She speaks for us both."

The man holstered his gun. "Sam. You keep your gun on the fella." To Quinn he said, "You look familiar."

"We've not met."

Casey heard edginess creep into Quinn's voice with his last comment. He offered nothing more, which further annoyed the other men.

"The lady." He motioned again for her to move forward. Once again, Quinn blocked her path.

"You will address my wife with more respect." Quinn took charge in a manner that both thrilled and annoyed Casey. She kept her own counsel to see how this might play out. Quinn shocked them all then by clasping Sam's pistol before anyone realized he had moved his hand. He flipped it as though he'd been handling a gun since infancy and steadied it on the others. "Now that we understand each other, I suggest you leave so we can get back to our work."

The men shared a quick look that betrayed their waning confidence but neither reached for another weapon. "What sort of work?" the tall one asked.

Events unfolded better than Casey had expected. "The kind we prefer to do in private. Excuse us." She took a bold chance by skirting around Quinn. She waved the others from her path. "The back door is still unlocked. Oh, and do not think to alert the marshal or anyone else. We prepared for such an eventuality. Can you say the same?"

Casey did not wait for a reply and passed by the men. Quinn remained on the other side, the gun still fixed on his targets.

"Wait."

She checked her smile before she turned around. "Yes?"

"Might be we could help you."

"Unlikely." Casey waited for Quinn's eyes to move in her direction. She held his gaze for a few seconds before walking down the hall and turning a corner. Her second purpose for coming here lay beyond the wall in the office upstairs, but they couldn't reveal the secret door to the others. If she was right, and she better be if she wished to assuage Quinn's anger, then their late-night criminal companions would seek them out.

She peeked around the corner when she heard Quinn speak to the men.

"You'll both forget what you saw here tonight."

The tall one spoke. "We're thinkin' you ought to be the ones to leave."

"Since I have the upper hand, so to speak, it will be you leaving." Quinn indicated the back door with a slight jerk of his head. "Time to go now."

"And you'll just let us walk on outa here?" Sam asked.

"Call it a gesture of goodwill among thieves." Quinn jerked his head again, this time adding, "Out you go."

Once the men were outside, Quinn closed the door and slipped the lock into place. Casey did not have to explain herself to him but reminding him once again that she was the Pinkerton would not mend fences. She also did not plan to tell Quinn he was right about posing as husband and wife. It afforded her more opportunity for cover than had she been on her own.

When she faced him in the hall, she expected a quiet reprimand at least. Instead, he returned to the section of the wall with the hidden door, clicked it open, and ascended the stairs. Casey lifted the hem of her long skirts to follow him up the dark passageway.

"You can take the office. I want another look at the map."

"Quinn."

"Yes?" His brow raised in the infernal way which spoke of his arrogance, yet at the same time made her feel like a chastised child.

Understanding crept into her thoughts. "You knew all along?"

"When our company made themselves known but not before. I assumed you wanted to return to this office. They were unexpected." He took three slow steps back toward her. "You expected them, though. Why?"

"You do not sound angry."

"Vexed is a better word for it, tempered only by my amazement."

"In what?"

He shortened the distance between them with one more step. "Are you hoping for a pretty compliment? I will gladly give it, for it is well deserved. You have a sharp mind."

"As do you. One cannot become both lawyer and bounty hunter without quick thinking."

"No, but the lawyer understands the need to carefully consider and plot before taking action. How did you know they would come here?"

He still stood far enough away so she did not have to tilt her head back too far to share a long, mutual stare. "Contrary to the credit you are giving me, I planned to only come here. It was when we were at the party that I thought perhaps the men at the cave might do the same. With Huckabee preoccupied, along with everyone else involved with Huckabee mining, they wouldn't have a better chance than tonight."

"The party gave you the idea?"

Casey nodded and moved to stand by the shelves and scanned the outer lip of each shelf for any disturbances. "Yes. Well, not the party itself, just what happened there. Huckabee was surprised when I mentioned progress, even after stating he expected it."

Quinn nodded. "I noticed. While suspicious, it does not make him guilty."

"No, it does not." An even layer of dust coated every ledge, except a narrow section of one on the shelf by the window. Casey leaned closer, careful not to disturb any more of the grime with her warm breath. "Suppose he is not involved. Suppose he knows nothing about the locations marked on the map in the next room. Well, that is surprising." She ran her finger along the spine of *Germinal* by Émile Zola. "No one would think to look here." Casey gently lifted the volume and slid it out.

"What are you doing?" Quinn's heavier footsteps sounded as he crossed the room. He examined the spine. "You read French?"

"Heaven's no, and I wouldn't read such a depressing novel if given the choice. No, my father had an eclectic library. If he worked on a case, he often read various texts—fiction or not—about the subject. I recall something about a coal company case but don't remember the particulars. It doesn't matter. The point is, this is probably a book no one would want to read, thereby likely to be ignored." Careful not to smudge the hardcover too much, she held one end of each side and shook the book.

Two pair of eyes followed the descent of folded papers. Quinn reached for them first. "I count four sheets." He scanned each one. "And none of the content makes sense. It appears to be a ledger but in a code."

Casey nabbed the papers from Quinn and studied them. "I think you're right, but . . ." Why did they look familiar?

"But, what?"

"I don't know." She slipped them down the front of her dress, and she felt heat rise up her chest and neck to warm her cheeks. Casey was used to getting creative while undercover, which often meant concealing papers, money, and even weapons beneath her clothes. "I did not bring a reticule." It was a weak argument considering Quinn's coat had pockets, but neither of them mentioned it. The slight lift of his mouth suggested he did not mind. "We can analyze this more later. Where are you going?"

"I told you. Since we're here, I'm going to get another look at the Colorado map." He lifted the bar from the door and entered the next room. "While I'm doing this, you can explain what about Huckabee's reaction led you to believe men from the cave would come here." Quinn glanced over his shoulder. "By the way, you don't know if those men *were* at the cave."

"A hunch."

"Mm. You have a lot of those." Quinn gave his eyes a minute to adjust to the darker space before focusing on the Durango and Silverton section of the map. Thanks to a clear night sky, moonlight penetrated the large windows on the second floor and illuminated the expansive work area.

"Why are you smiling?"

His finger rested just south of Hermosa. "What do you see?"

Casey brushed his finger aside and then understood. She also smiled but not quite for the same reason. Her hunch proved corrected. It appeared someone had attempted to erase the dark marking. They had also lightened three more of the markings, leaving only one remaining. "They *were* from the cave."

"Seems so."

"There might have been a lot more than engraving plates in those bags we found in the first cave. If they used these locations to stash more like those plates, and now those places have been erased from the map, then the caves must be temporary hidey-holes only. Whatever else they have, along with those plates, have been moved." Casey circled the last mark with her finger. "Except maybe this one. We might—maybe—retrieve something before they clear it out. All right, we should go now."

"We shouldn't have come."

"Are you sorry we did?" Casey allowed herself to be guided back into the smaller office because she was more interested in his response than in chiding him for his high-handedness.

"I'm sorry you're so stubborn and foolhardy *and* impulsive, but no, it was a productive outing. We could have come here in daylight. We have permission, and it helps to be seen. You take too many unnecessary risks." Quinn secured the bar, and this time, Casey took the lead and headed down the hidden staircase ahead of him. She did not, however, move out of the way when Quinn appeared behind her. She was fixated on the end of the hallway and the back door to the building which stood ajar, letting in the cool night air.

CHAPTER 19

Marshal William W. Wickline stood in the doorway's shadow, the lines of his dark suit visible with the help of bright moonlight creeping through the few inches between door and jam. His thick mustache twitched, though Casey could not tell if he moved any other part of his face. A light-colored Stetson sat atop his head, and the straight edges made Casey think it was a recent addition to his wardrobe.

Quinn, calm as anyone could be, eased her out of the way and closed the staircase door with a solid click. "Marshal."

The marshal bent his head in a slight nod. "Mr. Morgan." He then tapped the edge of it when addressing Casey. "Mrs. Morgan."

"Marshal Wickline."

Casey and Quinn shared a furtive glance with only their eyes. A measure of surprise shone in his at the use of the marshal's name for her. She would not underestimate Quinn's lawyerly side again. Did he not say lawyers considered and plotted carefully? Admitting to a sometimes impetuous and reckless behavior is not something she intended to do, though it may be true. She plotted and considered with the best of any lawman, lawyer, judge, or jury, but sometimes circumstances called for impulsiveness.

She had, after all, already met the marshal, and obviously, Quinn found time to also make the man's acquaintance.

"Now that we know we all know each other, why don't we have a chat." Wickline closed the door all the way, shrouding them in darkness. "When you came to me this afternoon, Mrs. Morgan, you failed to explain who you were."

Casey blew out a soft breath. "How did you find out?"

"Heard tell of a woman matching your description taking down Fletcher Jones recently. A Pinkerton agent by the name of McKenzie. They didn't give your Christian name or mention you were married." Before she could respond, Wickline addressed Quinn. "You, Mr. Morgan, are not in my jail only because you have some very influential friends. No, I haven't met him before today, but I recognized his name right off." His head tilted in Casey's direction. "Does your wife know?"

"Well, Marshal, she's not—"

"Your wife. Yes, I figured that out, too, though you've fooled enough people around town already into thinking otherwise, including the two sitting in my jail. They figured I ought to catch the actual thieves who might still be sneaking around

Huckabee Mining's offices." Wickline rocked back on his heels. "What are you doing here?"

A soft touch to Quinn's sleeve is all it took for him to not speak. "I had good reason for not revealing who I am to you, Marshal. The fewer people who know the better. I—we—cannot do our job if our identity is made known. We have only told Mr. Huckabee, and his assistant, Linwood, also knows, and now you. If word gets out, we will have a small group on which to cast blame."

Quinn smiled. Not that anyone could readily see it, but it came through in his voice. "What Miss McKenzie said."

"Why pretend you're married?" Wickline waved the question off. "Never mind. I'm sure you have your reasons. It doesn't sit well with me that Huckabee called you in to do what I couldn't."

"Why?" Casey moved a few feet toward him for a better look at his features. Quinn matched every step. "This case is not an easy one to solve, so there is no shame in it, and there is no reason to think you would not have solved it, eventually. Why, though, do you think so?"

Wickline chuckled. "What I've heard about you is true enough." He sobered. "I got as far as figuring that it had to be someone in Huckabee's employ, but not a single one of them said much, so there was no way to move forward. I reckon you found a way around the dam, so to speak."

"We did, or we think so." Casey saw on his face and in his mannerisms that her original supposition about the marshal was correct—he played no part in the crime or the cover-up. "Will you keep your silence and allow us to solve the case? After all, we are all on the same side."

"Interesting." Wickline directed his next words to Casey. "Did you intend to get caught?"

"Not by you."

"All right, then. You do what you must. I don't want to tangle with the Pinkertons, and I'd just as soon avoid hearing from one of his people. The telephone has been a nuisance ever since it came to Durango. People can't seem to leave things well enough alone." He rubbed a finger over his mustache. "If either of you gets caught by someone who shouldn't catch you, I'll have to run you out of town."

Since Casey did not believe him, she gave her agreement, and Quinn did the same after hesitating. Wickline muttered words neither of them understood and left them alone in the dark. She followed the marshal and closed the door behind her, hoping it slapped Quinn in the nose. Her soft-soled shoes carried her swiftly from the alley. Once out where someone might see her from a window, she slowed her steps a little but kept up a good pace until she reached the hotel.

The party showed no sign of waning, which suited Casey fine. The more noise downstairs, the less likely anyone would hear her yelling. Once at her room, she swung the door shut and spun around when it did not close.

"You want to explain what happened back there?"

"I really do not." Casey paused in front of the mirror above the dresser and assessed the woman staring back at her. She looked more like Cassandra McKenzie tonight, daughter of Alexander and Marian McKenzie, a city family from deep Scottish and Philadelphia roots and even deeper wealth. Transformation rarely bothered her because it meant she was doing a job. Looking like this, though, when it was not entirely a farce, discomforted her more than she cared to admit.

"Casey?"

She tugged two of the metal pins from her hair to let the lower half of her long locks fall loosely over her shoulders and back. For good measure, she wiped away the light bit of powder and rouge she'd applied earlier to complete her evening look. She felt more herself but wanted to step out of the dress and into a clean shift before slipping into bed.

"Casey?"

"I heard you." Casey walked to the foot of the bed and sat on the top of her trunk. "What did the marshal mean about your influential friends and when he asked if I knew?"

Quinn stared at her for several seconds before he rubbed a hand over his face once, then through his dark hair, leaving it disheveled. He picked up the single chair and moved it to set down in front of her. He lowered himself onto it and stretched out his long legs before bending both again and resting his arms on top. "I won't apologize."

"I didn't ask for an apology. I want an explanation."

"After law school and a stint as a city attorney in Boston, I joined the U.S. Marshals."

Casey studied him for any sign he might be holding back, but she saw no such deception. "Go on."

"I did not like some things I saw while working for the city, and I thought the Marshals would give me a place to exact real justice."

She shook her head, more in question than disagreement. "You did not find justice among them?"

He exhaled on a sigh and leaned into the back of the chair. "Some, but men's rules suffocated truth too often. I left on good terms and opened my law practice."

"How did the bounty hunting come in?"

"Accident or fate. To this day I don't know which."

Casey saw whatever he held inside pained him, and yet she offered no reprieve. She needed to know. "What happened?"

"The daughter of my second client was kidnapped. He was an important businessman, and wealthy, so he hired the best of everyone, including the Pinkertons. The Marshals were already after the man who took her, but they lost the trail in the Grand Tetons."

She suspected what came next in his story. "You went after them."

"She was twelve years old, Casey. Her father and mother doted on her, and they would have given all their wealth to get her back. No ransom came."

"Did you find her?"

He nodded. "A week after I set out with the best guide available at the time. Scratched and bruised, but otherwise unharmed. I almost killed the man who took her, and the entire time I thought justice would be served if I did."

"Except you brought him in."

Quinn nodded again, and Casey gave in to the urge to lay a hand over his.

"Her father had put a bounty on the kidnapper's head—dead or alive. He died in prison two years ago."

"You forfeited the bounty."

Surprise shone on his face. She shrugged. "A guess. A good one it seems. So, you are a bounty hunter who does not take bounties. That makes you what, a vigilante lawyer?"

"You disapprove?"

"No." And she sensed Quinn might not want to hear words of either sympathy or praise for his actions, so she kept those to herself. "How would Marshal Wickline have learned about you?"

Quinn splayed his hands before folding them under his arms. "I am acquainted with the governor, among others, and I don't use any name other than my own, so it easy to believe he's heard of me. Someone mentioned us to Wickline, though, before you introduced yourself."

"Governor of Colorado?"

Quinn nodded. "Decent man, questionable politics, and a

terrible poker player."

"Imagine that." Casey always considered herself well-connected, but if she ever found the law after her, she was glad to know a man like Quinn Morgan.

"Why did you go see Wickline? I assume this is before you dressed for the party."

"His jail isn't far from the telegraph office."

"You told him you were Mrs. Morgan, no first name."

Casey did not appreciate the blush that crept up her face. The curse of a fair-skinned redhead was the inability to hide even a slight color change. Undercover, emotion rarely got in the way. "Part of our cover. I had no specific purpose, nor did we speak much longer than two minutes before someone interrupted. I learned what I needed to tonight, though. He's not involved."

"I agree." Quinn rose and helped Casey to her feet. "Which is why it is time to take this operation to the next level. How long do you suppose before the Secret Service shows up?"

"Agent Johnson should have contacted them immediately after receiving my telegram. It is standard procedure in a case like this. I expect we have a few days before someone arrives."

"Plenty of time, at least I hope, for the next part of our plan."

"You mean the next part of the plan I have already devised."

Quinn's mouth twitched before he pressed his lips into a straight line. Casey saw right through him.

"I have it all worked out, Quinn. Hold on." She pulled the coded papers out from her dress and waved him over.

"Something about this looked familiar, but I was wrong about what. This third line of numbers here. It's the coordinates for Silverton, only backward."

Quinn did not hide his skepticism. "How could you possibly know that?"

"I've read a lot since we arrived and must have seen the coordinates somewhere." She shoved the papers at him and unearthed her map of Colorado. Casey smoothed it as she unrolled the map. "See, here. Huh. The numbers are off from the general longitude and latitude. Not much. Perhaps a specific location within the town or outside."

"It's not the location of the last mark on Huckabee's mining map."

"Mm. Well, it should be easy enough to find."

"Casey."

"Quinn."

He held her by the shoulders and turned her around to face him. "Were you going to tell me about this plan of yours?"

Casey delayed her response long enough to make him repeat the question. "Yes, tomorrow. I have a few minor details to finish."

"Have you not yet learned we work better together than apart?"

A thrill of shivers swept through Casey's body and over her skin at the double meaning behind Quinn's question. Of course, she conceded he may have been literal in only one meaning, in which case she needed to put distance between them—now. She solved the problem by walking to the window and looking out at the dark street below.

They were several hours away from watching the sunrise, yet Casey was not tired, despite her desire to crawl into bed. Her thoughts and eyes shifted to her sister's letter sitting next to the bed. She had not taken the time to read it yet and wondered how her sister's latest case was going.

Probably better than hers. Did Rose's friend, the dashing Dr. Whitman, cause her sister as much consternation and confusion as Quinn did Casey? Now she wondered if the good doctor *was* dashing. It was a word Rose might use. Casey finally kicked the unfamiliar cowardly behavior away and looked at Quinn. "Yes, I suppose in some things we work better together. I was not going to *not* tell you, but you made such a to-do about planning."

"All right. Tell me your plan." Quinn sat back down, a bold move for a gentleman to do in a lady's presence when she remained standing. But these were not ordinary circumstances, and the proper way of doing things did not seem to matter when they were alone.

"You will not like it."

"Assuredly."

"It will be dangerous."

"Perhaps."

"And it may not even work."

Quinn invited her to sit down, which she did not feel like

doing. When she shook her head, he leaned back again. "Why don't you start with what *it* is?"

Casey paced the length of the room and stopped in front of the woodstove. Warmth still emanated from the fire she'd built earlier in the evening while dressing. Quinn stood and moved in front of her. While he waited for Casey to speak again, he added two small pieces of wood and a few scraps of kindling to the stove and stoked the embers back to life.

"This plan is our best chance to see this done . . . and quickly before we're found out."

Quinn crossed his arms. "Every minute you delay in telling me is a minute longer I have to assume the worst. You want to ride into the den of thieves with guns drawn and show your badge? Or will it be more subtle? Perhaps you plan to play a harlot and seduce one of them into revealing all?"

"You place a great deal of confidence in my abilities to seduce a man." She wished she hadn't said the words the moment they passed her lips. "Neither."

He swung his arms out in defeat, letting them fall to his sides. "What then?"

"You're going to jail."

CHAPTER 20

"My plan was better."

"Your plan was going to get you killed."

"How is this an improvement?"

Quinn's gelding blew and snorted, eager to continue moving. "If you die, it won't be alone."

One thin eyebrow arched as Casey cast him a look of mild disapproval. Cool air swept over them, carried through the valley from the snow-topped mountains over acres of pine green mixed with muted golds, reds, and oranges. The peak foliage of the aspens had passed, but color still reigned for as long as nature allowed. Winter and autumn competed for first prize during the transition of seasons, but if the shift in temperature was to be relied upon as an indicator, winter would soon claim victory.

Halfway through summer, Casey always longed for autumn, and when the last of the colors faded away, she welcomed winter like a long-lost friend. When the bitter cold overstayed its welcome, she grasped onto the first signs of spring blooms. She measured her life and work by the seasons, with each bringing possibilities and annoyances. As much as she enjoyed the whitewashed beauty colder months brought with them, Casey needed the snow to stay above the tree line for a while longer.

The dry-packed earth beneath the horses' hooves, warmed already by the sun, suggested she might get her wish, but in Colorado, one could not hope that tomorrow would be predictable. No one had slipped a telegram beneath her hotel room door that morning when she awakened nor had one been waiting when she checked at the front desk.

Too exhausted from trying to get Quinn to see the wisdom in her plan, she failed to mask her disappointment and was rewarded with a curious look from the desk clerk. With her Colt secured at her hip and covered by a long, tweed coat, she mentally checked off the blade in her boot and the Webley Bull Dog in her pocket. She had fired the Webley, a gift from her uncle, only once when she first joined the Pinkertons. It had saved her life.

Ten minutes after waiting for him in the hotel lobby, Casey's patience withered. She almost went upstairs to pound on his door until she glanced at the clock above the front desk. There was a half-hour left before their designated time, and she did not hold out hope she could last.

Two minutes later, Quinn came down the steps looking well-rested. "Great, you're early. We have time for breakfast before we leave."

"No, we don't. Let's get going."

"We need to eat," he said as he glanced around to make sure no one was nearby. "Mrs. Morgan."

Any number of sarcastic retorts would have sufficed, but not a single one made it from Casey's brain to her mouth. "You better be a quick eater." She brushed past him and exited the hotel. However, she did not move fast enough to avoid the soft laugh behind her.

Four hours later, she and Quinn sat atop their horses, one-quarter mile from another mark on the map—this one less than three miles south of Silverton. She hoped there wouldn't be another cave since the last one nearly took their lives. She exaggerated, but it had been close—too close. Casey needed to learn to separate Quinn from the case. It was just another job, and once finished, she'd be rid of him. No more worrying about people who mattered, or could matter, which is how she liked things when on a case.

"Paisley is good to go, I think. If the men have similar stashes in each location, then it is going to take a lot more than the two of us to catch up with them. They may have already cleaned out the others."

"Paisley?"

"We are about to walk into what might be another life-and-death situation, and what I name the mare is what you take from this conversation?"

Quinn shrugged and calmed his horse with a few soothing

words. "I'm already aware of the danger. I did not, however, know you named the horse. You've become friends."

"She's named for the town where my father and uncle were born."

He appeared to be cataloging the information. "Your surname gave you away, but the random appearance of your second-generation accent makes sense now."

"Let us return to our present concern, shall we?" Casey saw the slip of a smile on Quinn's mouth before he straightened it out. "We are set on the plan, now, correct? I do not want to get there and have you change your mind—again."

When Quinn failed to agree immediately, Casey thwacked him with the tip of a leather rein. "Mr. Morgan."

"I like it better when you call me Quinn. *Mr. Morgan* always sounds like I'm about to be scolded, and I heard you."

"Either you derive a perverse pleasure from your impertinent behavior, or you are about to make me furious."

He did smile then. "As enjoyable as both of those sound, let's go with option three."

She closed her eyes for a few seconds and counted to five. She did not possess enough patience to count higher. "Which is?"

"We make for the cave."

Casey groaned. "Where?"

Quinn moved his hand through the air, starting at a stand of aspens, their leaves duller than the week before. "In the cliff, about a thumb to the left of those tall pines."

"A thumb?" She shook her head and sought out the cave in the cliff. "I see it, though barely. I suppose there is some wisdom in not trying to conceal the entrance. There are probably dozens of caves in this area that no one would bother to enter, and they found the most inconvenient ones. We'll need a ladder to get in there."

"I have rope, so we can find a way up and then climb down, or you can stand on my shoulders and I'll push you up."

Casey's narrowed eyes found a spot on the back of his neck where, if she hit it correctly, would knock him out long enough—

"Miss McKenzie?"

"What?"

"You keep losing focus. Where do you go?"

"I have excellent focus. As it happens, I was planning your murder."

"Mm. How did you do it?"

"Slowly." The mare accepted the gentle nudge of Casey's knees as her cue to move. She kept the horse to a brisk walk and kept a lookout for critter's holes hiding among the brush. Once they reached the cliff below the cave, she smiled. The cave opened a lot closer to the ground than it appeared from a distance.

Quinn dismounted and motioned for her to do the same.

"Do you have a dog, Mr. Morgan?"

He didn't reply.

"Do you have a dog, *Quinn*?"

"Not for a long time, why?"

"I will remind you I am not a dog to be commanded." Casey glanced back up at the opening. They had to see inside. Even if nothing came of the hunt, they needed to confirm if they were on the right trail. She felt they were. Down to her tiny investigator's toes, she knew it.

"My apologies."

Casey clasped a hand to her chest at his sudden appearance by her side. "Stop doing that."

"What?"

"You know what. You always just appear." She waved him aside and dismounted. Casey took more care to secure her horse properly this time by the shield of loose shrubs, though, they would be visible to anyone who might come upon the cave. When she faced Quinn again, a serious study of the entrance had replaced any trace of humor.

He hunched down and created a makeshift seat with his body. "Use my leg to stand on and you'll go right in." Quinn gave her his hand, and she accepted. "Ready?"

She nodded, and with strength and swiftness she wished she could not credit him, he lifted her up and into the cave with surprising ease. When she rolled and laid on her stomach to help him, he was already climbing over the ledge.

"Found a foothold in the rocks," he said by way of explanation. Quinn helped her stand but did not go so far as to help brush dirt off her clothes.

Casey studied the wide cavern. "What could they possibly have used this one for? It's not deep enough to hide anything. Oh."

"I smell it, too."

"This plan of yours might work a little better than we want. They won't want to leave evidence lying around for long." Casey followed the smell of decay deeper into the spacious cavern. Light filtered in far enough for her to see where each step landed. "Found him."

Quinn was already standing beside her. "This sight must be familiar." When she looked over at him, he added, "You are behaving remarkably un-female."

What was a female reaction? she wondered. Casey mentally counted the number of bodies she stumbled across during her career. She thought back to the first time, and how when she found a few private minutes alone, the retching began. The stench of death had remained with her for days after, so when had it become an accepted part of her life?

"I will fall apart and weep later."

"Will you really?"

"No." She leaned down to get a better look at the body. Quinn quickly pulled her back. "What are you doing?"

"Listen."

She remained still with his hands on her arms. Neither moved nor made an audible sound. "I hear it, though I wish it were whoever has been using these caves."

"You want a confrontation?" Quinn asked.

"I want the truth, and if a confrontation gets us to the truth faster, then confrontation there will be. We have little time before a full storm hits." Casey leaned forward again, and when she couldn't see the man's face from her angle, she nudged him with her foot. "Does he look familiar? His face has been . . . oh, my."

Quinn studied the man's face in the dim light. "Mr. Linwood."

Casey nodded as she tried to squelch the need to lose her simple breakfast of toast and tea. She was not as immune as Quinn supposed, which brought her tremendous relief. "He was one of the most unassuming men I have ever met. Dull is the word that comes to mind. What advantage does a person gain from killing someone like him? And what was he doing out here?"

"The obvious answer is he was involved."

"No." Casey shook her head a few times. "Men like Huckabee do not trust many people. If he held Linwood in as much confidence as he claimed, then I am going to assume the trust was not misplaced."

"I am inclined to agree, but finding him here confuses matters. This group—or the group the Pinkertons have been searching for—do not leave behind bodies, correct?"

"Correct. They're smart." Casey mentally reviewed what case

notes she remembered.

"They never leave behind evidence, no deaths have ever been linked to their crimes, and no witnesses, at least none found, which tells me either they are some of the best crooks alive or they—"

"Pay off any witnesses."

"I swear, Quinn. You finish my sentences one more time and you are going to get real comfortable with a gag." She raised both brows and stood firm and silent, daring him to call her bluff.

He coughed into his fist to cover a laugh. "Understood. Now, and I hate to admit this, but considering additional evidence, I believe we need to combine our plans."

"How so?"

Quinn looked at her sideways. "I will not go to jail if that is what you're hoping. No, this will be more complicated or simpler. Depends on how you choose to look at it."

Casey counted to ten this time. "I wish I did not understand you, but heaven help me, I do. We will need help, even if they don't know they are cooperating."

"Help will be appreciated. I am surprised none of your fellow agents have arrived."

The same niggling worry had occupied Casey's thoughts most of the journey to the final mark on the map. She should have heard immediately from her uncle, assuming he received the telegram right away. A telephone call would have been quicker, but Cormac McKenzie loathed phones and refused to install one in his home.

The telegram she sent off to Agent Johnson went to Colorado Springs, where he had informed her he would remain until she reported progress on the case. No word from either man unsettled her. She pushed those feelings back now to focus on the current situation. "No one can see us bringing his body back into town. They'll come back for him."

"I agree, but the man deserves a proper burial."

"He will get one. Once the marshal finds him—after we send a telegram from Silverton—he'll inform Huckabee, and they can transport him by train. We need to find out how Linwood came to be here, but we cannot get derailed from our plan."

A second thunderclap rent the air, and rain fell in heavy sheets when she and Quinn returned to the entrance. Casey shifted her thoughts from poor Mr. Linwood lying in the cave and gave the weather and their horses her consideration.

"This will not let up soon."

"We'll have to wait it out. Hopefully, it will calm down enough for us to make the last train out of Silverton." Quinn jumped effortlessly to the ground. "What are you doing?"

Casey sat on the edge and pushed herself forward. "I'm going to help you."

Quinn shook his head. "The horses are somewhat protected already. I'm going to see what I can do about a makeshift shelter, and then gather what dry twigs I can for a fire."

"We shouldn't need a fire."

"Just in case."

"Quinn." She gave him little choice but to hold out his arms to catch her as she slid easily into them. "Thank you."

"Stubborn woman," Quinn muttered as he left her side to go to the horses.

Almost everything on the ground was already wet, so she hunted up branches and twigs from beneath shrubs. Casey stumbled backward and dropped the stack of loose limbs she had gathered. When no sound followed, she sagged against the rock in relief.

"What's wrong?"

"Nothing."

"You're pale."

"It's cold." Casey waved to the thick bush. "A snake moved against my hand, or I think it was a snake. For a minute I thought rattler."

"Are you sure it wasn't?"

She nodded. "I've encountered one before, and they make their presence known. Besides, no bite." She held out her hands to prove it. "I hate snakes."

Quinn picked up the fallen stack of branches. "I found another cave around the side. Well, more of a carved outcropping. It's not deep. The horses are already in there. It will be cramped but will keep us dry." He led her past where they had first tied up the horses. The shallow cave was indeed cozy. She prayed an animal would not come along looking for shelter.

"There's enough daylight left for us to reach Silverton if this stops in the next couple of hours."

Quinn made a small pile of twigs near the entrance but away from the horses. He rooted through his saddlebags for matches, and after four strikes, ignited one twig with a flame. He glanced over at Casey occasionally to find she had not moved from her place by the mouth of the cave. She watched time press on as they remained stagnant. Not doing anything was her enemy.

Two hours later, Casey's soft-soled boots made tracks in the damp earth as she paced the length and width of the shelter. Quinn half-listened to the occasional mutter and sensed her patience had reached an unforeseen limit.

"This is why I work alone."

Quinn barely heard the words spoken from her clenched mouth. He did not need to touch her skin to know anger radiated from every cell of her body. Her face told him enough.

"*Your* plan would have put you here alone, and undercover or not, I refuse to go to jail for an idea that—"

"Would have taken less time."

It was Quinn's turn to be angry, and he didn't care how high-handed she might think him. "Is it really so bad to have someone help you?"

"You still don't get it, do you? I'm used to working alone."

"You've said as much. And you still don't get it—I'm not leaving you alone until this is finished, so imprint that in your stubborn head." Quinn didn't even know why they were arguing. The horses made little fuss at their temporary arrangement, yet with each passing minute, Casey's agitation grew.

"I'm sorry."

He almost pretended not to hear the mumbled apology. "You are a hard woman to figure out, Cassandra."

"I know." She dropped to the ground and held her hands over the fire. "You do pretty well. Figuring me out, that is."

"Not well enough, or I wouldn't always put your back up."

Casey stiffened. She must have realized it because she breathed out and relaxed her shoulders.

"What do you do when in Denver?"

She relaxed a little more and her shivering eased. "Take a lot of baths."

Quinn chuckled softly, then sobered when he saw she wasn't smiling. "You aren't joking."

"No." Casey tucked the edges of her split riding skirt under her legs, blocking any chance the cold air might have to make contact with her skin. "I travel so much, and the accommodations are never as nice as what Rose's house offers."

"Rose's house. Not yours?"

"Technically it belongs to us both, but I am rarely there, so I think of it as hers. The food is always amazing, the sheets clean, and the walls thick enough to block out sounds of the city." She shifted her seat a little. "I don't care for cities."

"You seem like someone who could adapt to any

surrounding."

"Out of necessity. I think about a permanent home sometimes, and when I do, the image is of tall grass blowing across rolling hills with the mountains so close you think you can touch them. Rose seems to thrive in Denver with her experiments and all the goings-on gives her plenty to investigate, but after a week of being there, I just . . ."

"Can't breathe?"

Her eyes met his. "Right. I can't breathe. It's better than Chicago, though, where my mother and uncle live."

Quinn did not press for details, not when she was offering information about herself. He wondered so often about the Cassandra McKenzie he had first met in Colorado Springs, then later, a woman dressed in men's duds at a bar in Durango. "Why did your uncle think you would make a good Pinkerton?"

"I don't know that he did exactly. He helped me because I asked him to. My mother fought it . . . thought it inappropriate work for a woman. Rose and I, our father . . ." She listened to the rain falter and ease its torrent. "We should be able to ride soon."

Quinn waited for her to continue talking. Instead, she kept silent for several minutes. Quinn returned to his horse and withdrew a muslin cloth from his saddlebags. When he sat back down, he unfolded the cloth and offered her some of the jerky. "It's good. The wife of a rancher outside Colorado Springs makes it."

Casey accepted one of the thick strips of dried beef and took a bite. She immediately pounded her chest as a round of coughs escaped. "You could have warned me," she gasped.

"I figured you for someone who likes a little spice."

She coughed a few more times and waited for her eyes to stop watering. "Spice yes. This is," she took another tentative bite, this time prepared, "cayenne, and a lot of it."

Quinn's grin disappeared only long enough for him to take another bite of his own strip. "It wakes a person."

Casey cleared her throat, studied the meat, and braced herself before tearing off another small piece. She managed not to cough the third time. "I wasn't asleep."

"You were something."

She scooted a couple of feet and braced her back against the stone wall. "On my third case, another Pinkerton with even less experience than I had got this idea about being in charge since he was the man. I mostly ignored him because the job came first, and we were close to catching our target. Then he figured he wanted to be a hero. It didn't matter what I said, he wasn't going to listen to me."

Quinn guessed what happened to the Pinkerton. He waited for her to tell him.

"We were after the worst sort of person. He killed a young family on their farm and escaped capture for three months. My partner—if one can could him that—and I were supposed to draw him out. The killer ended up dead, and so did Agent Tuffin."

CHAPTER 21

"I'm not him."

Casey brushed dirt from her clothes to keep her hands busy. "If it's just me, and I end up hurt or dead, then I have no one else to blame. The responsibility of a partner is too much."

A long stretch of silence passed before Quinn asked, "What was your second worst case?"

Casey did not try to hold in the unexpected chuckle, and after it slowly died down, she regarded him carefully. "Thank you. As to the second-worst case, it involved tracking down a stolen ballgown."

"Now *that* is a joke."

She shook her head. "It's true. A wealthy society matron from New York was in Salt Lake when a gown she had specially made in France, and delivered for the governor's ball, was snatched. The seamstress tasked with making final alterations at her shop fainted when I questioned her. I suspect she was more afraid of the matron than of me."

“How did the woman get the Pinkertons to take the case?”

“When the local police failed to locate the dress, and the U.S. Marshals refused because, and I quote, ‘We don’t look for missing ballgowns,’ the woman’s husband reached out to the Pinkertons.”

Quinn tossed two more branches on the low-burning fire. “Why did you take the case?”

Casey sobered. “It came right after Agent Tuffin’s death. A ridiculous job sounded grand.” Another laugh bubbled up. “We found the dress.”

“Since you appear to be ready to burst, skip ahead. Where did you find it?”

“Onstage.” Casey’s wide smile reached her eyes this time. “The owner of a dancing hall took it for his principal attraction. The woman had no idea the ruckus her fancy dress had caused.”

Quinn chuckled softly and asked, “What did the matron say when you told her?”

“I thought it best to tell her they had ruined the dress beyond repair. Fire might have been mentioned.”

“And?”

Casey grinned unapologetically. “She fainted. After that, I insisted on having a say in which cases I accepted.”

He marveled at her ability to reach within and find humor despite her earlier revelations. She was, in his estimation, the most grounded person he’d ever met. “An odd concession for the Pinkertons to make.”

"They concede or quit, and I somehow convinced them they needed me more than I did them. They learned quickly what cases I preferred, and the work remained challenging."

The rain eased to a trickle before it stopped. Gray clouds soon dissipated until a sky of powder blue backdropped a brilliant white sun whose rays finished nudging the last of the clouds from its reach.

Quinn stood and held out a hand to help Casey up. Once on solid footing, he released her and stomped out the fire before scooping dirt and dropping it on the last of the embers. They were both relatively dry now, and the sun would finish the rest before they reached Silverton.

He met her outside where she'd led the horses into the sunlight. The brief storm heightened the autumn colors and transformed the landscape from dull to vivid. A fresh dusting of snow scattered across the mountains and topped the golden trees at the lower elevation. Quinn wondered if Casey's lined duster was warm enough to ward off the cooler chill now saturating the afternoon air.

"We can't leave him."

"I know." They returned to the cave where Quinn passed her his horse's reins, found a foothold in the stone, and pulled himself up. Once on solid footing, he called down, "Will you toss me up the blanket from Raider's saddle?" Once Casey did, he added, "Bring Paisley next to the rock, just below here. I won't be long."

Quinn returned five minutes later with Linwood's body wrapped in the blanket and hefted over his shoulder. It took careful maneuvering to lower Linwood onto Paisley's back. Casey guided the man's lower body while Quinn held onto his arms until he hung over the saddle.

He climbed out of the cave and secured the body with rope. Once done, Quinn held out his hand to Casey. "Raider is strong enough to carry us both to Silverton."

She sat behind him with her arms wrapped around his waist. Her confidence on a horse did not extend to riding double, and the precarious position on Raider's flank meant her grip remained strong. Quinn did not mind in the least. Casey had yet to explain to him how she intended to accomplish the least dangerous part of her plot once they reached the mining town. Her lack of willingness to share information concerned him on their quiet ride the last few miles to town.

Hundreds of residents and tourists filled the streets and various establishments of the booming town high in the San Juan mountains, with even more men—bachelor and family alike—scattered in the mines and on small homesteads, all doing their best to eke out a living on land unforgiving of the weak. The panic of 1893 decreased output from the mines, though no amount of economic depression stood in the path of those willing to scrabble their way through to the other side.

He could not fathom how people in this high-mountain town got through the last winter, with temperatures among the coldest ever seen in Colorado. His work took him more often to cities where amenities made life easier during the Rocky Mountains' most difficult periods. From determined expressions that spoke of stubbornness, he suspected fortitude was chief among the traits one had to possess to start a new life here.

Of course, such places also made good temporary homes for criminal elements. How many lived and worked among the good folks of Silverton? Quinn asked himself. He had no interest in drawing attention from anyone—criminal or not—and guided their small party away from the main road. Quinn spotted the undertaker's building set away from the others and stopped in front.

"I will only be a minute." He helped Casey slide off before dismounting. A minute later, as promised, he exited the building with a stocky man of average height, a thick red beard, and brown eyes that looked weary around the edges. "I explained to Mr. Sligh here how we came across the body. He'll look after him."

"You don't know him?" Mr. Sligh asked.

"We don't," Quinn said. "But I will cover the cost. No one should be left to die as he was."

Mr. Sligh rubbed his thick beard. "The marshal will need to be told."

"He will. You have my word." Quinn untied the rope from around Linwood. "I'll help you bring him inside."

Once back on their own horses and headed back to town,

Casey tucked her long braid beneath the collar of the duster, and she eased her hat down farther over her forehead. Quinn doubted anyone who got a good look would mistake her for anything other than a beautiful woman, but no one they passed appeared too interested. A few of the men ahead of them waved to men and women standing out front of businesses.

They pulled in behind a group of six men on horseback, allowing themselves to get lost in the mix in case anyone might wonder about them. When the riders drifted toward the livery, Quinn counted themselves lucky. He and Casey put a few yards between them and the other men and waited for the riders to conclude their business with the livery worker and walk away.

"Help you, mister?"

Quinn surveyed the tidy stockyard. The horses in two corrals appeared clean and water in a large trough reflected the sun. The yard would not do such a good business if they weren't trustworthy. "We need to board our horses for a few hours."

The man looked over Quinn's chestnut gelding and the pretty Palomino mare. "Stable or corral?"

Quinn withdrew enough money for two days' worth of boarding and handed it to the man. "Stable, if there's room. Fresh grain and water, too."

The man eyed the money, smiled, and nodded. "Ain't no one better with horses in these parts. I'll see to 'em myself."

"Thank you." Quinn noticed Casey remained behind her horse, out of sight, and did not speak when the man led their mounts away. "All right. You want to explain how this is going to work?"

Casey gave her back to two new arrivals at the stockyard. "Meet me out front of the Grand Hotel in thirty minutes." She unhooked a flat pouch from her waist, took out a few coins, and pressed the pouch into his hands.

He hooked her arm with his as she walked away, forcing her to half-spin around. "Where are you going?"

"The Grand in thirty minutes."

"Casey."

She slipped from his hook. "No place you can go without a lot more of these," Casey said, waving the coins in the air.

Quinn watched her walk away and disappear behind a passing wagon loaded with mining tools. He swore and started to follow her. Twice he headed after her and twice he changed his mind. She wanted him to trust her, so he'd give her that.

Thirty-one minutes later, he pondered on how many hotels, laundries, and saloons he'd have to upturn before he found her. There had been time enough to send a telegram to Marshal Wickline about Mr. Linwood, but notifying the local marshal would have to wait until they concluded their business. Their cover depending on no one seeing them do anything suspicious. He perused both ends of the street twice more before checking his pocket watch. Thirty-two minutes.

"You'll scare folks off with such a fierce scowl."

"I'm sorry, ma'am, I . . ." Quinn tolerated surprises as a

natural part of life, not to mention the unexpected that comes along with lawyering and bounty hunting. He preferred, though, fair warning from those with whom he entered into working relationships. Had Casey—no, she looked like a Cassandra right now—given him some notice, his words would not presently be caught in his throat. "Where? How?"

"Money is often the simplest and quickest solution to a problem." Her sultry accent held hints of Charleston and Boston, confusing the listener as to where she might be from, but offering no doubt of her genteel and citified upbringing.

He continued to stare at her until she lightly kicked his shin. "Still the same Casey. Good to know. For a minute there I wasn't sure." Quinn gave up trying to figure out how she managed such a transformation in so short a time. He admired her wide-brimmed hat with lace at the band, her fitted bodice, all the way down to the hem of the printed silk and velvet dress.

"It is a few years out of style and more suited to mornings, but I doubt very much anyone we meet will notice."

No, Quinn thought, they won't notice the dress, but they most certainly will notice her. "That shade of gold is most becoming, though I am partial to red."

"Are you?"

He nodded and presented her with his arm. "It is a recent discovery of my preferences. Where are your riding clothes?"

"With the woman who loaned me this dress. She allowed me use of her room to change."

Quinn did not want to ask, yet the question came out. "A room where?"

"Have you heard of Blair Street?"

The forced stop landed them in the middle of the busy road. Two riders and a wagon moved around them while Quinn stared down at her, dubious about the possibility. "That ensemble did not come from a gambling house or bordello."

She urged him to keep walking, and while they kept a leisurely pace, they veered to the side of the street where they blended somewhat into the crowd. "In fact, it came from Madame Lucy's Sporting House. Apparently, the girls there cater to a more discerning clientele and dress the part."

"How did you know you'd find what you needed there?"

"I hoped, and research always helps." When Quinn's raised brow indicated he didn't quite believe her, she added, "I overheard one of the serving girls mention Madame Lucy's that night at the saloon in Durango."

Quinn navigated them out of the path of a passing wagon. He said nothing, but a smile remained on his lips when they reached the land office. He opened the door and allowed her to enter first. The door closed behind them and blocked out most of the noise from town. Despite the smaller population, Silverton's locals and visitors operated at a higher decibel than those in Durango.

A wiry woman wearing a tidy, white apron over a black dress hovered over documents behind one of two long counters.

Shelves and drawers filled the length of one wall. The woman glanced up, not pleased about the interruption. Her dark eyes matched her raven hair pulled back in a severe knot at the nape. "May I help you?"

"We hope so." Quinn kept a hand in the center of Casey's back as they stood by the counter. "My wife and I are looking for a mining office."

"A lot of those around here. Which one in particular?"

"Pitt & Tate. We understand they are no longer in business but hope to speak with someone who worked there. Do you have information on the previous owners?"

Casey nudged Quinn's knee with her own, and he returned the signal with a gentle squeeze at her waist. Neither of them had missed the flash of interest in the woman's eyes. "Smith & Sons now occupies their old office. One falls and another is quick to take their place. One street over. You'll see the sign. Can't say you'll find who you want."

The woman dismissed them by turning back to her papers. Casey might have overlooked the woman's renewed interest in her work were it not for her surreptitious glances every few seconds. They were about to leave when Casey slid her hand into the pocket of Quinn's vest and removed the folded certificate they took from Huckabee's office. She returned to the counter and waited for the woman to look up again.

"Was there something else?"

“Yes.” Casey laid the unfolded certificate on top of an open ledger. “Is this your work?”

CHAPTER 22

The bell attached to the door of the land office jingled when it opened to a newcomer. The woman tore her startled gaze away to focus on the question being asked of her. A few minutes later, the gentleman left, and the clerk locked the door. She turned the simple wood open sign to closed.

"Who are you?"

"Mr. and Mrs. Penrose. Now you."

Her frantic eyes darted back and forth between them. "Molly."

When Molly added nothing else, Casey gave a single nod. "Very well, Molly. Is this your work?"

"I don't recognize it."

Quinn tapped the top of the certificate. "My wife asked you a question, Molly."

"Why do you want to know?"

"Could be whoever managed to create this fine work might be interested in more . . . work." Quinn retrieved the paper and tucked it back into his vest pocket.

"Who are you?"

"My wife already told you, though I understand your concern. Given the nature of our inquiry, you realize we cannot tell you anything else until we are assured you are the person we seek."

"Who sent you?"

Casey caught the subtle heightening of Molly's voice, and how the other woman folded her arms to cover up wiping the palm of each hand on her sleeves. Casey took another leap. "Sam."

At once, Molly's shoulders relaxed and she flattened her palms on the counter. "Sam never mentioned anyone named Penrose."

"We met Sam in Durango last night. One might say we all ended up chasing the same treasure."

Molly eyed Casey with greater interest now. "You don't look like anyone Sam would know."

Casey's slow smile was genuine. "That is the idea."

Quinn had enough of the questions. "Are you wasting our time, Molly, or was Sam right about you?"

"What do you want?"

"Your work is exemplary. Better than anyone else we've hired before. We want more of the same and can pay handsomely for it."

The tip of Molly's tongue darted out to lick her lips at the mention of money. The woman lacked the skills of a master criminal, Casey thought. No one adverse in the art of subterfuge revealed so much with their face. The money mattered to her a great deal, though. She wondered how submerged into trouble Molly had to have been to fall in with the likes of the criminals they were chasing.

"All right then," Molly said. She glanced at the closed door. "You'll have to come back later."

"Here? At closing then," Quinn said.

"No." A fine sheen of perspiration formed on Molly's brow again. "There's a cabin half a mile south of town off a dirt road. It's not marked, but there's a tall pine and a massive boulder next to it. You'll see the cabin half a dozen yards in." Molly skirted the counter and ushered them out. "You have to go now."

Quinn refused to move yet. "Are you planning to double-cross us, Molly? Perhaps tell the marshal?"

"I swear on my mother's grave." Molly flipped the sign and unlocked the door. "Please, before someone else comes in."

They walked to the next street, arm in arm before they found a quiet place free from passersby. Quinn led her to a bench placed haphazardly against the side of what appeared to be an empty building. He righted the bench and invited her to sit down.

"This is a borrowed dress."

Quinn's right brow shot up. Casey met his fierce gaze straight on.

"All right, don't sit. Tell me how you knew it was her."

"You didn't suspect?"

"Her? Of being the forger?" Quinn shook his head. "Of knowing someone from Pitt & Tate, yes. How did *you* know?"

"A guess."

"You guess a lot."

"You asked before why my uncle thought I would make a good Pinkerton. Well, that is why."

"Meaning, when you guess, your assumptions are more often than not proven correct."

Shouting between two men close to where they stood became raucous laughter and faded away. "Uncle Cormac thought it a useful skill."

"It is. However, as a lawyer, I can tell you that courts require evidence beyond instinct."

"Which is why we're going to meet Molly in the cabin and hope we aren't riding into an ambush."

Quinn's lips curved up at the corners, the smile of a man who held a secret. "If it is an ambush, it will be on them, not us. Now, where is Madame Lucy's Sporting House? You, my dear, are far too overdressed for what I planned."

Sagebrush, rocks, and dirt do not a soft bed make. Casey grumbled a little to herself, careful to keep her discomfort from Quinn, who laid on his stomach as though twigs were not digging into him. She owed the difference to the thicker fabric of his clothes. "The one time I do not wear a full corset."

"What did you say?" He lowered the binoculars she had brought along.

"Nothing." She rolled from side to side enough to tug on her duster and bunch it up beneath her. "Molly has ten more minutes to arrive before I head back to the land office."

"You can't solve everything with threats and a gun."

"True, but sometimes those are more efficient. We have already missed the train back to Durango, and now she is late."

"Your new friend probably has rooms available at Madame Lucy's for the night if we need them." Quinn cocked her a grin and took the light cuff she landed on his arm. "Last I checked, women with your background were not brought up learning how to properly punch."

"Women of my background rarely become Pinkerton agents, yet here I am." To explain, Casey added, "The first man I arrested showed me."

"Mm."

"It is true."

Quinn looked at her then, clearly unbelieving.

"He did not realize what he was doing, but I learned all the same. It has come in handy a time or two. I still prefer my Colt." She swiped the field glasses from him and peered through the lens. "We have guests."

"More than one?"

Casey's nod did not properly translate from her position.

"Two. Molly and a man dressed like a banker." She passed him the glasses. "Does he look familiar?"

Quinn studied the man carefully. "He was with the group who arrived at the stockyard in Silverton before we did. He's changed his clothes."

"Do you remember if he saw you?"

"Unlikely. He wasn't paying attention to us, and we held back far enough while they left their horses." Quinn stood and helped her to her feet. "There is only one way to find out if this will work."

Casey brushed briars from her duster. Storm clouds rolled in to block what remained of daylight. "Let's get this done before the weather turns and we end up trapped in this cabin with our new friends. It is growing cold enough to snow up here."

They waited for Molly and her companion to enter the cabin before hiking a short distance down a slope that gave them a good vantage point. Their horses were tied to a hitching post behind the boxed, log structure and shifted where they stood when Casey and Quinn walked up alongside them.

Rather than enter through the rear, they made their way to the front and entered through the open door. Molly's surprise showed clearly in her already frazzled expression. "You're late, Molly." She gave the other woman a few seconds to grow used to Casey's changed appearance. Loose ringlets from the wig fell from beneath her own Stetson. It cost her another five dollars to keep the hairpiece and worth every cent. "You brought a friend.

We dislike surprises, Molly."

The man in question pushed back his wool jacket to reveal a shiny black leather holster with a pearl-handled pistol.

"This is Levi. He's my partner." Molly leaned close and whispered too softly for either Casey or Quinn to hear. Whatever she said mollified her companion enough to cover the pistol again.

Casey half-expected Quinn to take over the conversation, but for whatever reason he kept silent. Energy vibrated through the air in the cramped quarters bereft of chairs, so they all remained standing. A scarred table stood in the center of the room and an oversized cot was pressed against one wall while a wood stove in the corner might offer warmth when lit.

She invited Molly and Levi to move closer to the table. "We won't keep you longer than necessary. We need shares certificates created for two different companies."

"How much?"

Casey addressed Levi. "We pay well."

"How much?"

"How much do you want?"

Levi named a price. Molly gasped on a soft breath.

"We pay well, but we are not fools and this is not our first time." Casey moved to leave when Molly called out.

"Wait." She named another price.

Casey put her back to the pair and leaned close to Quinn while he kept watching them. She whispered, "Say nothing. Are they looking at us?"

Quinn nodded.

Her hand moved up his arm in a gesture meant to distract the other two. "He is the one to introduce us to the leak in Huckabee's office."

Quinn nodded again.

"Good." Casey said the last louder and faced the others once more. "We accept your price."

"Do you have the certificate samples with you?" Molly asked.

"We won't be needing those. They were merely a way to confirm who you are. No, what we require is far easier and of much more importance." Casey placed two sheets of paper on the table. "One is a sample. The other is the letter we need to have penned. Can you copy the writing exactly? It has to be precise."

With shaking hands, Molly lifted and examined both. She gaped when she read the words to be copied. "This . . . I'll be hanged!" Her shout came out breathy.

Casey waved away her concern. "Not hanged. We four are the only ones who know, and we certainly will not tell anyone."

Her partner took and read the documents. "She'll do it."

"Levi!"

"Quiet woman." He shoved the papers back at Molly and said to Casey. "She'll do it, but the price has doubled."

Casey pretended to consider the new ultimatum until Levi slowly revealed his holster and gun again. "Very well. Double, but I expect it done by morning. We will come by the land office."

Molly shook her head with far more force than was necessary to get her message across. "No one can see us together again. We can meet here."

Quinn finally spoke. "Out here, alone, carrying your payment. I think not. The land office tomorrow when you first open, or we leave now."

Levi and Molly huddled. Molly's shout of "No!" earned her a pinch to her left arm. Casey had to hold up an arm to keep Quinn from advancing. "Do we have a deal or not?"

"We do," Levi said. "We're leaving first." Levi and Molly passed on the opposite side of the table to reach the front door.

"Levi, no last name." Quinn blocked his exit. "If I see a single mark on her tomorrow morning, you'll be getting more than money from me." He grabbed Levi by his starched white shirt and lifted him up and onto his toes. "Do not cross me." Quinn let go and Levi stumbled back. Once righted, he sent a glare to Quinn before pulling Molly along with him.

Once the two riders were out of sight, Casey and Quinn returned to their horses. She looked at the now-empty path and sketched both Molly and Levi into her mind. "Does Molly seem familiar?"

Quinn helped Casey onto the mare's back and swung up into his saddle. "I have never seen her."

"Neither have I. Something in her eyes or maybe the color of her hair." Casey ticked off faces in her memory bank one by one and stopped halfway through. The face she most needed to see did not appear except as a blurred figure. "I know her from somewhere."

"Or she looks like someone you know. Considering the trouble she is into, it would not surprise me if she has a relative somewhere—"

"I've got it! Burton Amos. I swear on my future grave that Molly is kin to Burton Amos."

CHAPTER 23

Quinn counted himself blessed that never in his adult life did he have to escort a sister, betrothed, or wife to the dressmakers. The sheer number of fabrics, underclothes, dressing gowns, stockings, corsets, and ribbons were enough to make a man kneel in thanks for being born a man.

He silently rattled off many excuses he could have used to get out of venturing into Silverton's sole modiste's shop to procure Casey a nightgown for that evening and a dress more suited for the train ride home in the morning. She insisted neither was necessary, which stirred many images in Quinn's mind of what she might wear to bed otherwise. He ignored her, and after securing the only suite left at the Grand Hotel, left her alone to no doubt scowl at his departing figure.

Now, he wished Casey had offered more insistence. Like a man staring into the lights of an oncoming train, he froze as he scanned the interior of the shop. The modiste took pity on him and offered to show him a selection of dresses and bedclothes.

"My wife is a few inches taller than you and slender. We weren't expecting to be here overnight. Whatever you have for a nightgown and a suitable traveling dress already made will suffice for the short journey."

The woman gaped at him, then came back to herself and cleared her throat. "Very well. What is your wife's coloring?"

Quinn almost said "blond," but the golden locks were temporary. For some reason he did not wish to dwell upon, he wanted the dress to match *her*. "Red hair. Sort of red, like a burnt sunset. Blue-gray eyes."

The modiste smiled in understanding. "Come with me."

She showed him the dresses first. Any of them would have suited, until she showed him a dress of simple lines, edged in lace, in almost the same shade as Casey's eyes. "I'll take it."

She smiled again and held up three nightgowns. Quinn did not know why it mattered what Casey wore to bed, but when he saw the white linen gown cut at a curve on the bodice, with long, flowing sleeves, and ties instead of buttons up the front, he nodded.

"My nephew will deliver these."

Quinn gave her a single nod and withdrew his pocketbook. "The Grand Hotel. You can leave them at the front desk. The name is Morgan."

"Very good, sir. Your wife may return in the morning if the dress needs to be fitted better to her frame."

He remembered Casey's frame well enough to know the dress

would fit. If it didn't conform to her body perfectly, she wouldn't care. "Thank you for your help." Quinn paid for the items and left the shop. The hotel stood as grand as its name across the way. For a rough mining town, Silverton attracted its share of fine ladies and gentlemen, though what they did this high in the mountains, Quinn did not bother to guess. Money and scenery, he supposed, were two good enough reasons.

Early stars winked in the darkening sky as sounds of boisterous revelry seeped from various establishments. Quinn took stock of it all and ignored the entertainments to be found among the miners, gamblers, and working girls in favor of the quiet suite where Casey waited for him.

When he unlocked the door to the suite, he found it barricaded.

"Casey."

Part of her face appeared in the narrow opening. "There is only one bedroom in this suite. Find another."

"There are two beds, and it is the only one available." He interrupted her before she spoke. "I am not sleeping with the horses, in a sporting house, or under the stars, so put the notion out of your head."

The door closed with more force than necessary. Quinn heard some scuffling and grunting on the other side before it opened once more, though not all the way. The chest of drawers still blocked part of the entrance, so Quinn squeezed through. "How long did it take you to move that from over there?" He pointed to where light drag marks appeared on the carpet.

"Not as long as you might think."

"Dramatic."

"I was making a point."

"Then I missed it, unless you intended to really keep me out, in which case I will leave and you may exert your impressive force once again to move more furniture."

When he did not follow her into the room, she looked over her shoulder. "Now you do not want to come in? Please, make up your mind."

He stared at her. "You're wearing a shift."

"Yes."

"And nothing else."

Casey lowered her face to take in the same view as Quinn. "Indeed, I am not." She crossed the room and took down a robe from a hook next to the chest of drawers. Certain there was not an inch of skin without a warm blush, Casey kept her back to him. "Now I am."

"Where did you get the robe?"

"The clerk at the front desk is quite adept at his job. Apparently, anything one wants, and if it is to be had in this town, he can get it. Or so he claims." She smoothed her arm over the sleeve. "It feels new."

"You were not in the least bothered by it."

"By what?"

"Your lack of attire."

"I cannot account for it, except to say I am getting used to you and did not think of it. I had only just finished my bath." Probably too used to him, she thought. "Might we discuss something other than my bedclothes?"

"Why did you block the door?" Her heavy sigh joined a look that told him he should have guessed. "All right. You blocked the door since you were taking a bath and did not trust you would hear me enter or that I would be smart enough to figure out I shouldn't. But once done with the bath, you decided to make me aware—for the last time—that you can take care of yourself, and you did this by showing me you did not need help to move a heavy object all by yourself."

"Rather long-winded. You were right to the first part, wrong to the second. I forgot to move it back after the bath. Really, how does moving furniture prove anything when you are already aware of what I can do?"

Quinn gave up. No amount of energy was worth digging himself out of whatever proverbial hole followed the convoluted conversation.

"I meant, why don't we discuss something useful, such as where you have been for the past hour."

Quinn's smirk held untold secrets, and he was not inclined to share them yet. As much as he wanted to continue to admire the loose copper curls piled on her head or the way the wrapper both enveloped and enticed, he tore his gaze away. "You sound like a nagging wife."

"And you like an obstinate husband. Lucky for us both, we are not truly married."

"More's the pity."

"What did you say?"

"Nothing important." Quinn dropped a parcel wrapped in brown paper on the bed closest to the door before he removed his duster, jacket, and vest and rolled up the sleeves on his dusty white shirt.

"You're in my bed."

He gave her a wry look.

"I will remind you that you are a gentleman."

The soft laugh surprised him as much as her. "So I am, and as much as I enjoy your indignation, I am taking this bed because it will be between you and the door while you're sleeping."

Casey cast a glance to the door, then back to the bed. By silent agreement, they both ceased speaking about the bed. "You did not say where you were for an hour."

"Before the modiste—never wanted to add that word to my vocabulary—I learned a few things about Molly."

"The modiste was unnecessary, and I, too, learned something of Molly."

Quinn stopped in removing his boots. "The less you are seen around town, the better. We agreed."

"I never left the hotel."

"Am I to surmise that you have found a suitor in the hotel's clerk willing to go about town at your bidding?"

She lifted her shoulders in a dainty gesture and took a seat in one of the plush chairs. "Assume what you will. There is also a general store downstairs, which is most convenient. I assume it is where he got the wrapper. What did you learn and from whom?"

It was Quinn's turn to feign indifference. "Her name, before her marriage to Levi Vaine, was Molly Amos, family unknown."

"Hmm."

"You learned something different?"

Casey returned from her wayward thoughts. "No, Molly Amos, same as you heard. Curious, though. I did not take her for any leadership role in the criminal enterprise. If Burton Amos traveled here to help her or to help someone she knows, then she may play a bigger part than I believed."

"Is it curious because you may have been wrong about her?" Quinn set both boots, heels first, against the foot of the bed.

"Odd because I am not generally wrong." Casey glanced his way. "Sorry. That sounded far more arrogant than I intended."

Quinn lay back on the bed with his feet still on the ground and laughed.

Casey rolled her eyes at him and told him, "The bathwater may yet still be warm. Who told you about Molly?"

He nodded his head toward the other room in the suite. "Is the bath in there?"

"It is, and you are avoiding the question."

"Your friend at Madame Lucy's has proven helpful in many ways." Quinn remained fully clothed until he was in the next room with the door closed.

Casey watched the closed door, waiting for it to open again. There was no need to hide her amusement, and she kept her laugh soft enough not to be overheard. Were she the jealous sort, and if she had reason to be jealous, she might have taken Quinn to task over his deliberate attempt to make her green-eyed over . . . what was her name? Ah, yes, Lana of Madame Lucy's and the borrowed morning dress. "Not her real name," Casey murmured aloud, and then thought how much her sister would appreciate such a tale.

She read back over the letter she finished before Quinn's arrival, crumbled it, and started over.

Dear Rose,

Have you trounced anyone lately? There is great appeal to not only investigating but as you would say, "trounce the culprit." Do you really wish you could be a part of that? The arrest, I mean. Odd how you should speak of envy, for I have often thought the same of your work. You have no one to answer to besides your conscience, and we both know it is far more angelic than my own.

This case is vexing, and I find myself at odds with half the decisions I make. I blame Mr. Morgan's influence. If I was alone—as I prefer to be—I would carefully think over each choice out but with no one else to offer an opinion.

Even Agent Johnson does not give as much input on a case as this man, and yet, Mr. Morgan has proven more valuable than I expected. Is it the same with you and Dr. Whitman?

I had hoped Frank Huckabee would be the only victim in this case, but another has surfaced. The cold, calculated side of me sees it as one less person to investigate, which is hardly a kind way to think of the poor man. Do you ever think it odd how we have spent our lives? Mr. Morgan asked me why Uncle Cormac thought I should be a Pinkerton, and it made me think back to the early days when I first joined. Would Father be proud of us?

Goodness, this talk is maudlin, and I haven't time for that. Christmas this year should be special and hopefully quiet. Perhaps Mrs. Pennyworth could make her special clootie dumpling. My mouth waters every time I think of her spiced pudding. Would you hint at it next time you talk of the holiday?

Mother's letter that you mentioned still hasn't arrived, but she wouldn't have known to send it to Durango. It is probably languishing in Colorado Springs or Cheyenne. I think that is where I was when I last sent her a telegram. If she is coming before Christmas, I am most curious as to why.

Back to the case. I expected excitement with harlots, miners, and murderers about, but a quiet evening with my feet up and one of Mrs. Pennyworth's special teas sounds divine right now.

There is movement in the next room, which means Mr. Morgan is about to return. We have a busy night ahead of us. Oh, dear, that is not as it sounded. I promise to explain everything when I see you next.

For now, I have to go and trounce someone.

With anticipation to try those bath salts.

Lovingly, your sister,

Casey

Casey folded the letter into an envelope and set it aside to post tomorrow, and set a fresh sheet of paper in front of her and drew two circles in the middle. From there, she slid the pencil along the sheet to form various lines and assigned each one a name. Burton Amos was no longer a problem, but why was he in Durango if not to help his sister? **Molly Vaine** warranted a line of her own as the forger, but Casey still did not think she was a direct link to the leader. Perhaps she felt threatened and her brother was meant to offer protection. Casey ignored the speculation and moved on to current players in a game that grew more frustrating by the day.

She stared at the paper. The only two people she cared about were the ones in the middle who they had yet to identify. Casey wrote two more names down: **Ellison Huckabee** and **Agent Johnson** with a question mark next to each one. Until she found proof to absolve them, or evidence against someone else to wipe out suspicion of them, she had to consider all possibilities.

Next, she wrote **Pritchard, Nutting,** and **Percy**. She met them only once at the party, but everyone was suspect. She circled Pritchard's name because as the accountant, he had the most financial knowledge about the company. Then there was Mr. Nutting, the mine manager, whose surprise was more obvious than the others when they mentioned a desire to purchase Huckabee Mining.

"Not enough to convict the man," she said aloud. "He could fear for his job." The same could be said for any of Huckabee's employees. She added Levi's name to the list, next to Molly's. She drew a square around Levi's name. He looked as familiar as Molly, but she had yet to figure out why.

At the top of the list, she wrote, **How did the man at Huckabee Mining connect with the thieves?** "Forgers do not advertise their services," she said aloud.

The knob rattled on the door to the bathing room and Quinn stepped out, having exchanged dirty clothes for a clean shirt and pants. The shirt was open halfway to reveal a clean union suit beneath. She glanced at the bed and found the brown parchment parcel was no longer there. "You did a little shopping for yourself. I imagine those will not be comfortable to sleep in."

"With you in the same room, they will have to be comfortable enough. What were you saying as I came in?"

"I said, 'Forgers do not advertise their services.'"

He trailed fingers through his damp hair and looked over her shoulder to read the question and the list. "So how did they meet? Well, that is the question. Not a lot of names on there."

"I have already dismissed half of the people we've encountered since our arrival, so they are not worth the trouble. These are the ones who matter most now." Casey touched the tip of the pencil to Molly's name and the two empty circles. "We will confirm Molly as the forger in the morning when we see the results of her work. If she proves to be the one we're after, we need her to lead us to the person in Huckabee's office who betrayed him, or at worst, to her contact who then leads us to the inside man."

"It won't be a long list." Quinn brought another chair over, sat, and looked around the room. "Dinner should have been delivered by now. I asked for it before I came up."

"They do not bring meals to the rooms."

"I paid them plenty to overlook their rule." Quinn pointed to the paper. "Without Molly, we'll have no proof against the man or woman disloyal to Huckabee. We'll need her testimony or a confession. Both are better, but without a confession, a witness is necessary."

"Which is why we are on this ridiculous chase through the mountains to find our forger. How many people in Huckabee's office would have access to the necessary material? Unless they did not need the information or at least not all of it."

Quinn laced his fingers over his taut stomach and leaned into the back of the chair. "You're thinking more than one person in the office?"

"No. I am thinking of one person who made others believe he had the authority of others." She dropped the pencil and leaned over the edge of the table. "With Molly's talents at our betrayer's disposal, it is not unreasonable to assume she has forged many documents for him."

"It could be another woman. We weren't expecting the forger to be one, after all."

Casey shook her head. "The way Molly does her husband's bidding, and how she was more nervous of you than me when we first met tells me she is more likely to follow a man's lead than a woman's."

"Let us say you're right."

They sat for several seconds in silence while Casey waited for Quinn to say more. "And?"

"I'm thinking." Quinn pushed himself out of the chair and paced the room twice. "I think better when I'm not hungry. I'm going to go down to find out what happened to dinner and will bring food up myself if necessary." He sat on the bed and pulled on the first boot. With his foot halfway into the other, Quinn lowered his leg and let gravity do the rest.

"I do not need—"

He held a finger to his lips and slowly rose from the bed. He motioned for her to go into the bathing room. Casey's response was to retrieve her Colt from beneath the pillow on the bed she first intended to occupy. Quinn did not bother to rebuke her. Every bit of his focus was on the door. The knob did not turn, and shadows did not pass over the light seeping from their room into the hall. Still, someone waited or watched. A chill swept over Casey's body, raising the hair on her arms and the back of her neck as she held the pistol at the ready.

CHAPTER 24

Quinn rotated the key as quietly as possible and opened the door at the same time someone slipped a large envelope through the narrow opening beneath the door. Quinn pulled Molly into the room, careful not to step on the envelope.

"Start explaining." Quinn kept his gun lowered but did not set it aside. He shut the door against anyone else who might be nearby.

Molly raised her hands and kept them up when she started blabbering. "Please don't be angry . . ." Her eyes darted to the gun. ". . . or shoot me. I brought what you wanted." She moved one finger only to point to the envelope.

Casey put her gun away and came forward. With both hands, she pushed Molly against a wall. "This wasn't the plan."

"I know." Molly's eyes filled with the first sign of tears. "You have to leave."

Casey let Molly go and dragged a chair to the middle of the room's empty space. "Sit down and explain."

Molly did and dropped her hands to her lap. "If you look, you will see I brought exactly what you asked."

Quinn bent to pick up the envelope. He handed his pistol to Casey before he withdrew three sheets of paper. The first was the original document with the handwriting sample, the second the text they wanted copied, and the third was a perfect duplicate of writing style and letterhead design. "Extraordinary work." He waved this in front of Molly. "How did you get it done so fast?"

Molly bit her lower lip and shook her head. "It's done, isn't it? You should leave town now."

"The train doesn't run at night, as you know well enough." Quinn set the documents on the chest of drawers. "Unless you want me to send for the marshal—"

"You won't!"

"Don't test me." Quinn hunched down in front of her. "None of us want the marshal to know about our arrangement, but I prefer to deal with him than with Levi. Look at me, Molly." When she met his eyes, he asked, "Levi does not know you're here, does he?"

Molly shook her head, the unshed tears finally falling. "He means to take the money for himself. I need that money."

He stood up straight. "Where is Levi now?"

"Blair Street. He'll be there all night."

No doubt gambling away funds he had yet to receive, Quinn mused. He and Casey exchanged a long, studied look. Neither of them needed to verbalize what the other was thinking. Casey gathered clean clothes and retreated to the adjoining chamber.

"Molly, look at me. Do you know where on Blair Street?"

"He has a few favorite places." She shrugged. "Could be any of them depending on what he's after."

Quinn silently translated that to mean depending on his preference for gaming, drinks, or a warm bed with company. Casey stepped back into the room carrying the robe after changing into a black shirt that buttoned up the neck, a dark, wool riding skirt, and a matching vest. She was dressed to move about in the dark. When she sat on the edge of the bed to pull on her custom boots, Quinn spoke to Molly while Casey secured her knife in its sheath. "Molly, listen. Can you help us with one more task?"

She bit her lip again and kept her focus on Quinn even though Casey now stood next to him. Quinn remembered what Casey said about Molly probably fearing him more than she did Casey. It was not his intention to frighten the poor woman any more than necessary, but with the end within reach, he had little choice.

"What else do you need?"

"You'll be compensated for your trouble."

With the promise of more money, Molly nodded.

"Good. Do you know anyone at Huckabee mining? Or anyone else involved in these schemes, other than Sam?" Casey moved behind him, out of Molly's sight, and pinched his arm. He ignored the light sting. "Molly?"

Her skin lost color, which she could ill afford to lose. "I don't understand."

"You do, Molly. You understand well."

She swallowed air in a loud gulp. "Who are you?"

"I don't know what mess you're in, or how deep it goes, but we can help you get out." Quinn looked over his shoulder at Casey, met her eyes, and conveyed with a look what he dared not say aloud. The choice had to be hers.

EVERY DECISION INFLUENCED the next and the consequences of each decision were often predictable. Once in a while, a result of significance surprised her, and none more so than the influence Quinn now wielded on her choices. She would never compromise truth or justice for the sake of any person. With Quinn, she knew such an outcome would never be a concern, for a man of his integrity compromised no one.

She accepted his unspoken request and circled him to stand in front of Molly. "Do you want out? A new life, far away from here, is possible."

"If I help you."

Casey thought of the badge in her satchel; what it meant to the Pinkertons, to her, and in the centuries-old fight of right versus wrong. In the greatest of all battles, right wins out, even if some might consider the choice wrong. "No." She took a deep breath and said again, "No. The help is yours no matter what comes next."

Molly cupped her face in her palms and released a stream of sobs. Casey lacked the gentleness required to comfort a person in the throes of dramatics, and while she believed in the sincerity of Molly's relief, tears often discomforted her. "Molly?"

The other woman slowly calmed and her crying trickled to a few sniffles. "I'm sorry."

"No need to be sorry." Casey met Quinn's gaze. She did not know when words ceased to be required for them to communicate.

He nodded once, took a small velvet bag with a drawstring from his trunk, and handed it to Molly. "Your fee, for work completed."

Mouth agape, Molly held tightly to the bag and felt the unmistakable bulge of paper bills and coins. "This is—"

"Double the fee, as instructed. It's all yours, Molly, and you can leave to live whatever life you want, away from your husband." Quinn walked toward the door.

"Wait!"

True to her word, Casey would have let Molly walk away, even aiding her out of Silverton on a train to anywhere she longed to go. She was, however, grateful for the insight that told her Molly's resolve to see this through outweighed her fear.

"I met one man from Huckabee Mining Company, once, when Sam introduced us."

Sam again, Casey thought. She guessed he still languished in

Marshal Wickline's jail along with his tall companion, who remained nameless to them. "Anyone else?"

"A man named Carney. I didn't hear his first name."

"Did he work with the man at the mining company?" Quinn asked.

"None of them did, except Sam."

Casey wanted to leap across the mere two feet separating them but held back her excitement. "What do you mean by none of them?"

Molly twisted the strings on the money bag and inched forward in the chair. "The men who work with Levi. They've nothing to do with Huckabee Mining."

"Then how did they know to take the payroll?"

Molly's expression of genuine bewilderment at the question. "They helped, of course, but it wasn't their plan. They have rules."

"Such as never leaving a body behind."

Wide-eyed and trembling at the mention of dead bodies, Molly said, "Yes."

Casey ticked through a mental list of possibilities based on the new information. If they were to believe Molly's accounting, then no one in the forgery and theft ring was responsible for Frank Huckabee's death. What then of Mr. Linwood? "Thank you, Molly. As my husband said, you owe us nothing more."

Molly rose from the chair while twisting the money bag. "I can come with you."

Quinn and Casey said nothing beyond what their expressions conveyed, and since both remained stoic, neither gave away what they thought of her suggestion.

"You can use the skills of someone like me, can't you?"

"You'd trade one master for two?" Quinn asked.

"Perhaps a partnership."

Casey shook her head. "We do not accept partners, and we still do not know if we can trust you."

"What if I showed you?"

Quinn nodded to the chair for her to take a seat again. "Show us how?"

"The men Levi works with, well, I think they're growing tired of him. I heard Sam say they wanted new people who could help them expand."

Casey sat on the edge of Quinn's bed. "Go on."

"I can introduce you to them."

"My wife already said we don't take on partners."

Molly licked her lips and gripped the velvet pouch tighter. "They don't take on partners either. The job you're planning with the letter I did, well, they can help. It's a big job."

Casey stood and dragged Quinn to the far side of the suite, while she kept watching Molly. She stepped as close to Quinn as possible so as not to be overheard. "I still only care about finding out who killed Frank Huckabee, and it doesn't sound like anyone in this group did it."

"I agree, but they could lead us to whoever did. We know

there had to be someone in Huckabee's office involved, someone with access to payroll, banking, and delivery information."

"Anyone working there with enough motivation could have gotten the delivery schedules, and payroll is simple enough to figure out. A person wouldn't need banking reports to pull off the theft." Casey jerked her head in Molly's direction. "I have no doubt she is the forger, and her skills are indispensable to the people behind the theft and Frank's death."

"They won't let her walk away."

"Exactly what I was thinking."

"But you still want to use her."

Casey tilted her head back a fraction to meet Quinn's disapproving look. "If she wants to do this, then yes. If she doesn't, then she walks away, we go back to the mining office and force everyone to stay there until we get a confession."

"It won't work. The culprit will keep quiet, or worse, cast blame elsewhere, and we'll waste a lot of time."

"Precisely, and the murderer is in that office. As a lawyer, you know we need proof, a credible witness, or a confession if the courts have any chance at a proper conviction."

Quinn rubbed a bit of the tired from his eyes. "We can't stay here tonight."

A wide grin spread across Casey's face. "I have an idea."

"Why do I feel that I will not like it?"

Casey raised her shoulders in indifference and returned to Molly. "All right, Molly. You can come with us. Do you have a safe place to stay tonight, where Levi won't find you?"

She slowly shook her head.

"Then you may stay with us. Do you live far from here?"

"No."

"Good. Gather what you want to take with you tomorrow and meet us behind the hotel in fifteen minutes." Casey walked Molly to the door. "Will that be enough time?"

"Yes, and thank you."

"Do not thank us yet." She opened the door and checked the hallway for any signs of people and finding none, stepped aside. "Fifteen minutes."

Molly rushed down the hall toward the stairs, all the while clutching the velvet money pouch to her chest. Casey waited until the other woman was out of sight before she closed the door and walked back to the center of the room.

"I know that look already. You're not sure what is bothering you, but something is."

"A lot of things are bothersome about this case." Casey collected her few items from around the suite and stuffed them into one side of her saddlebags while Quinn secured the documents from Molly in his.

Ten minutes later, they stood in the alley behind the hotel. Casey planned to give Molly only the agreed fifteen minutes before they left. Any longer and trust became an even bigger concern. "You're certain the horses are okay for the night at the stockyard?"

"I took care of it." Quinn lifted her saddlebags from her arm and draped them over his shoulder with his own. "We'll collect them in the morning and be on our way the minute the train leaves."

"Well . . ."

Quinn nudged her chin, so she'd look at him. "Well, what?"

She shrugged and peeked at Quinn's watch again. "She has one minute."

"Even my patience has limits. What have you planned that you aren't telling me?"

Casey smiled. "Quite a lot, if I am to be honest."

"And you're always honest."

She neither confirmed nor denied it. "Fifteen minutes. Let's go."

No sooner did they step out of the shadows did Molly turn a corner and hurry down the alley. The arm holding a large carpet bag flayed as she tried to keep the bag from bumping her leg.

Out of breath, she came to an abrupt stop a few feet from them. "I had to wait for my neighbor to leave."

Quinn held out his hand for her bag. "I cannot in good conscience allow a lady to carry her own bag."

Molly sucked in deep gulps of air and smiled. "Thank you, but I'm stronger than I look."

Quinn shrugged as though doing her the service did not matter, but Casey saw suspicion flash in his shaded eyes. Casey led the small procession on a zigzag course to the road behind

Blair Street and stopped at the back door to Madame Lucy's Sporting House.

"Well, at least you don't disappoint."

"How is that?" Casey beckoned Molly to enter first and waited for Quinn's response.

"I knew I would not like your plan."

CHAPTER 25

"Where is it?"

Casey contemplated the one bed in the room Lana offered them for the night. She confessed that Madame Lucy died the year before when she stepped between two angry customers fighting over their favorite girl. Her heart stopped right there in the middle of the argument, but she ended the fight. After fifty-five years in the business, Lana said it was time for Lucy to quit anyhow.

The girls who worked there now ran the sporting house, and Lana delighted in naming her price and accepting the coins Casey discreetly handed her.

"The money."

"I am torn between telling her we aren't married and need two rooms and sending you out there among them to fend for yourself. Lana enjoyed the look of you."

Since Quinn had given little thought to their would-be hostess for the night, he ignored the comment. "What you do with your money is none of my concern, but since you seem to have been carrying around far too much of it, you put us both in danger."

She tugged her saddlebags off his shoulder, bringing his with them. The added weight took her by surprise, and she dropped both on the bed. "I don't plan on sleeping tonight, so I suppose one bed or two doesn't matter." Her face grew hot when she realized what she had said. "I only meant that sleeping on a bed where . . . that has been used . . . you know what I mean."

"It happens I do." Quinn chuckled, though she failed in diverting him from the earlier question. "How many people have seen you open your purse since we've been here?"

Casey yanked open one of the leather flaps and withdrew a bar of soap, a toothbrush, and cleaning paste she bought at the hotel's general store. She sighed and stuffed the soap back in the bag, for she could not hope for a bath in the morning. "Have I told you the number of cases I have worked on during my time as a Pinkerton?"

"You have not."

"Twenty-two cases. Most were over quickly, but still a respectable number." With brush and paste in hand, she walked to the washstand, made sure the porcelain bowl was clean, and poured in water from a pitcher. "Lana assures me they use this room for the most discerning of clients. That does not ease my mind. Yes, twenty-two cases, and not once during any of those did someone attempt to rob me."

Casey could not bring herself to clean her teeth in front of Quinn, no matter how mundane the task. She found him sitting on the floor with his back to the wall and his legs spread out in front of him. "Have I bored you to death?"

His lips twitched. "I somehow doubt you capable of such a feat." He opened his eyes. "Boring is not a word I would ever associate with you. I was merely waiting you out."

"The location of the money is such that I cannot show you right now. Suffice to say, it is safe. I keep only a small amount in the pouch at my waist."

Quinn allowed his eyes, now alert, to drift over her body.

"Don't look at me like that."

He closed his eyes again. "Pondering the possibilities. The chair doesn't look much more comfortable than the floor but should suit for a few hours. We'll need to move again at first light."

"About that." Casey closed the distance between them and knelt on the ground next to Quinn. "We will need to purchase another horse."

He briefly opened one eye. "Why?"

"For Molly." Quinn's sigh was exaggerated enough to flutter strands of her hair. She scooted back a few inches. "We can't very well rob the train if we're on it."

Quinn gave her his full attention. "We're not robbing the train."

"Of course we're not, but what Molly doesn't know . . ."

He braced himself against the wall and climbed until he stood straight. Without speaking, Quinn lifted Casey to her feet and held her in place with light pressure on her shoulders. "I swear, Cassandra, if you live to be thirty it will be a miracle."

"You used my full name. You're angry again aren't—"

Before she could get out the last word, Quinn's lips pressed to hers in what some might call a savage kiss, except it was too brief to be called savage and too long to be called brief. She agreed with her rambling mind on one thing—she wished he hadn't stopped. When he set her away, she simply stared at his chest. It took her a few seconds to raise her eyes to his face. She said nothing.

"Good to know I found a way to render you speechless." Quinn grabbed his duster and hat and headed for the door. "Now, I'm going to find us some dinner."

Several minutes passed before Casey regained her composure. She crossed to the window, opened it all the way, and stuck her head out to take in the frigid night air. Soft flakes fell from a dark sky, blocking the stars' glimmering light from reaching Earth. Her eyes closed of their own volition, as the cold brought her back from where Quinn had dropped her on a cloud of confusion.

When her eyelids fluttered open, she felt more like the version of herself who made a living on the back of justice. Had she not returned to herself, Casey might have missed the shadow of a familiar woman two stories down beneath the window. She looked down at her clothes and wished she had trousers. Casey picked up her long coat off the bed, grateful she'd left Durango with the dark one. She searched the cozy room and found scraps of paper and a pencil to scrawl a note for Quinn.

Five minutes later, she stood outside and searched the busy road for a sign of Molly. Blair Street did a brisk business well into the early morning hours, though most patrons were inside one of the many establishments. She glimpsed Molly slip between two buildings and planned to follow until Levi emerged from one of the sporting houses. He raised an arm into the air, splashing liquid from the bottle he carried.

One of the other patrons yelled at him to quiet down when he started singing. The man was tone-deaf. She did not hold out hope that even drunk, he would not somehow recognize her. Casey circled the building until she reached the next street. Molly was nowhere to be seen.

Her sister always said of all the virtues to have skipped Casey, patience sat at the top of the list. She proved Rose right after fifteen minutes of searching when she gave up.

Casey sneaked into the shadows and ventured back to Madame Lucy's. When she entered their rented room, she found Quinn sitting at the small, round table in the corner with a variety of food spread out. He leaned back in the chair, crossed his fingers over his stomach, and trailed her with his gaze as she walked toward him.

"I'm ravenous. Where did you find anything decent to eat at

this hour?" Casey plucked a slice of bread off the cloth Quinn had set beneath their meal.

Quinn released his relaxed posture only long enough to pass her the note she'd left him. "'Be back soon' is not an explanation."

"I followed Molly."

"To where?"

"I lost her a few buildings down. Levi stumbled out of one of the sporting houses." Casey bit into an apple wedge. "He appeared drunk."

"He could have still recognized you."

"Which is why I avoided him and lost Molly."

Quinn passed her a glass of water. "This is the only clean glass Lana found before she had to tend to a client. Molly cannot be too afraid of Levi if she went out alone tonight. Did it appear as though she was looking for him?"

"I don't think so." Casey drank a third of the water and gave the glass back. "More like she didn't want anyone to see her. She indicated gambling and drink are his weaknesses, so perhaps she wanted to make sure he got home safely, but I doubt it. Wait! The gambling." She dropped a second apple wedge before it reached her lips. "Could it be so simple?"

Shouts and jeers in the hall interrupted them, followed by what sounded like a man's body connecting with a wall. The grunts confirmed it. A woman's shriek joined the cacophony.

"Who thought finding shelter in a whorehouse would be so

noisy.” Casey’s face burned red at Quinn’s raised brow. “Never mind. You know what I mean.” Chiding herself, she reached for her holstered pistol beneath the coat she forgot to remove when she entered the room earlier.

“Uh-uh.” Quinn went from sitting to standing faster than Casey could pull the Colt from leather. “You’re not going out there. Neither of us is getting in the middle of two men fighting over a woman.”

She appreciated that he said “woman” instead of “‘whore,” and oddly wondered if he had ever availed himself of such a female. The scuffle continued to where Quinn reversed his thinking and headed for the door. “You are not going out there, either, Quinn. If—”

A bullet splintered the door and pierced Casey’s flesh. Quinn caught her when she slumped forward, forcing them both back into the chair. Together, they crashed to the floor, with Quinn taking the full force of her weight.

THE DOOR BURST open and Lana, fierce and sporting a bloody lip, rushed into the room. A woman continued to scream in the hall, and for now, it seemed, the gunshot had quieted the brawling men.

“Were you hit?”

Quinn shook his head and felt along the top of Casey’s back until he found the wound. “Casey?” He gently rolled her to the side and knelt over her. "Casey!"

"Quiet down out there, Marcy!" Lana yelled at the loud woman in the hall. "If you aren't screaming like that for pleasure, then there's just no sense in it." She asked Quinn, "What can I do?"

"I need fresh water—warm, if you can manage it—and clean cloths. Does this town have a doctor?"

"He's away. Told me when he was here two days ago. Don't expect him back 'til end of the week."

Quinn swore and put more pressure on Casey's wound. "Can you get into his office?"

"The marshal can."

"Good." He noticed her bloody lip for the first time. "You're hurt."

Lana swiped at the blood. "I tried to get in the middle of those two fools."

Quinn thought under different circumstances, Lana and Casey might have a few things in common. "I need a needle, thread, gauze if the doctor has any, and the strongest alcohol you can get."

Lana hurried to do his bidding.

"And close the door!"

Quinn did not know who obeyed the last demand, and he didn't care. He refused to let strangers gawk over the bloody scene. Alone with her, he breathed deeply, set aside the near-crippling fear, and focused on Casey. He kept one hand on the entrance of the wound and felt the front of her shoulder. No exit.

"So help me, Cassandra, you *are* going to live." He skimmed every visible surface and saw nothing to soak up the blood. Careful not to jar her too much, he released pressure long enough to use both hands. He removed her arm on the uninjured side from the sleeve of her duster and tucked the excess beneath his knees. He then slid the blade from her boot, untucked her shirt, and carefully sliced through the fabric of both her vest and shirt.

Once he had a good hold, he put the knife aside and ripped the materials up the center of her back and used the cut pieces to cover the wound. Blood seeped into her white, linen shift beneath.

The sound of someone fumbling with the door preceded Lana's entry into the room, burdened with a bowl of warm water and a short stack of different colored cloths. "This is all we had." She set everything down next to Casey. "The marshal went to the doc's."

Quinn traded the bloody shirt and vest scraps for a cloth. "You found him fast."

"He was down the hall." She left the rest unsaid. "Took care of those two buffoons who were fighting over Marccy. Happens once a month when they come down from their mining camp. We're happy to take money from the lot of them, but some just don't have a lick of sense."

Quinn listened with little interest, except to use Lana's voice as a distraction.

"How can I help?"

"Are you squeamish?"

Lana shook her head.

"Good. Hold down here." He grabbed one of her hands, placed a cloth in it, and pressed it over the wound beneath Casey's cut clothing. "I'm going to remove the rest of her clothes that are in the way. Don't move your hand until I say."

"Shouldn't we move her to the bed?"

"I don't want to risk shifting the bullet."

Lana stared at him. "Are you a doctor?"

"No." Quinn stood and washed his hands in the porcelain bowl at the washstand. When he returned to kneel by Casey, he removed her coat completely. Quinn took up the knife again, cut away the rest of her vest and shirt, and eased the remaining scraps from around and beneath her.

"You sure you know what you're doing? Might be I could find—"

"No!" He glanced at Lana. "Sorry, no. I've seen this done."

Lana replaced the bloody cloth with a clean one. "Never asked her what she wanted that wig and dress for yesterday."

Quinn did not appease her curiosity as he lifted Lana's hand long enough to see the wound.

"Your wife seems like a real strong lady to me. I'm sure she'll be fine."

Yes, Quinn thought, his wife is the strongest lady he's ever known.

CHAPTER 26

One does not forget the first time a horse threw her into the air. Casey's recollection of that childhood disaster when she soared over the feisty thoroughbred's head, tumbled over the long grass on her grandfather's estate, and landed on her back filled every painful thought as she slowly regained consciousness.

If she had only known way back then what she knew now—it is the men who always get you into trouble. Her reflections on the past brought to mind the present, specifically Paisley, the gentle mare who would never throw Casey from the saddle. An image of Raider filled her thoughts next, and soon Quinn replaced everyone and everything.

"Quinn!"

"I'm here." He sat next to her on the bed and brushed hair from her face.

"The shot. Were you hit?"

"No. You were. I hoped you would stay out until we reached Durango. How do you feel?"

"Like I've been shot." Casey tried to stop her head and body from spinning until she realized movement all around her caused the sensation. "We're on a train."

"Yes, though I daresay it's no longer worth pretending to rob it. Care to explain now how that plan was supposed to unfold?"

She lifted her head from the soft pillow and looked around. "Where did you—"

"One of Pullman's finest. Why did you want to rob the train, Casey?"

"I already explained it wasn't going to be a real robbery. It was part of the plan to draw out Levi's associates."

"Seems an overly complicated way of achieving the goal."

"We might have caught more of them." Casey wished now she was still asleep. "Where did you get the Pullman?"

"An investor at one of the mines was visiting Silverton, and I prevailed upon him to loan us the car. It took all the money both of us had left, even though he didn't need the funds."

"You could have told him who I really was. People like the Pinkertons." She swallowed to moisten her dry throat. "Most people anyway." Quinn held a glass of water to her lips and she drank her fill. "Thank you. What happened to Molly?"

"She's in the parlor section. This morning she was waiting at the train when I brought the horses around so they could go into the stock car. I rode in one of these Pullman coaches before, but nothing quite like this. Pullman knows luxury." He put the glass aside. "A buffoon shot you—Lana's word for him, not mine.

Lucky for him, you lived through it or he'd be the one in the ground."

"You wouldn't have killed him." When Quinn did not respond, Casey clasped his arm. "What happened to him?"

"He is sitting in the Silverton jail and will be sent to Denver for trial. I told the marshal who you were and asked him to keep your identity quiet for a few days."

Casey groaned and lay her head back on the pillow. "He might not, which means we have little time to find the killer. As to that, I think whoever killed Huckabee also killed Linwood, and I am certain he is not part of the band of thieves Molly knows."

"We'll talk it all over soon. You should rest for now. We will be in Durango in forty-five minutes."

"Which is why I don't have time to rest." Pain cascaded up her arm when she shifted in the bed. "Who removed the bullet?"

Quinn rose and pulled back the curtain from the window. "The doctor was out of town, and I didn't have time to find another."

Casey digested the information, grateful it had been Quinn and not a stranger. "Where did you learn?"

"A tracker I used once got a bullet in his leg. The closest doctor was crude but efficient. I watched."

"I'm glad you did. Thank you."

Quinn nodded and unable to stand or sit still, paced the small area next to the bed. "Molly gave me a few more names she's heard Levi mention. None of them work for Huckabee."

"Did she say where she went last night?"

"I haven't mentioned you followed her, and she has said nothing about it. I'm not entirely certain we can trust her."

Casey considered getting out of bed. She wiggled her toes to make sure everything from the waist down worked, and that led to her reaching under the quilt to feel her legs. "All the money you and I had left. That's what you said before." Casey lowered the quilt and looked down. "Where are my clothes?"

"The ones I cut off you went into the fireplace at Madame Lucy's. Your skirt is in your saddlebag. The modiste delivered your new dress and nightgown to the hotel as instructed. I'd forgotten about them until I passed by her shop this morning and she came out to ask if I received them." He pointed to a large rectangular box. "They are there when you're ready."

"That's how you found the money pouch."

"Strapped to your thigh. Ingenious."

"Unless one gets shot and it is discovered." Casey deliberated between her choices of embarrassment and common sense. If Quinn was not going to be bothered by the intimate act of stripping her down, neither would she. Mostly, she clarified.

"Lana dressed you."

Casey's head shot up. "Lana?"

Quinn nodded. "While the prospect of undressing you held immense pleasure, I would never do so without your permission. I noticed the pouch through the fabric of your shift. Now, had a capable woman not been available . . ." he shrugged and left her to fill in what remained unsaid.

"I am grateful then, to you and Lana. She proved to be a friend, after all."

"She did."

Casey pushed up on her elbows, then collapsed under the weight. Quinn rushed to her side and helped her sit up. He used the pillows to keep her upright. "You are behaving like a caged animal who can't break through the bars."

"You could have died last night, Cassandra."

His eyes met hers. The depth of emotion she saw in them pushed her beyond comfort and reason. Except for her family, or more precisely, her sister, no one, to her knowledge, ever cared so deeply. Even her sister's occasional concern for her safety, and sisterly love, did not compare. Unable to process the revelation when there was still much work to be done, Casey avoided a direct response.

"Thanks to you and one of Silverton's finest madams, I am alive."

The glib remark earned her a disappointed look. Quinn's jaw tightened for a few seconds before he spoke again. "I will be sure to recommend her. If you will not sleep, we should discuss what will happen when we arrive in Durango."

WITH MOLLY'S ASSISTANCE, Casey donned the dress Quinn

purchased in Silverton. She had yet to ask him what prompted the purchase of both dress and sleeping gown when she said neither was necessary. Both were of fine quality and in styles she might have chosen for herself. She smoothed her fingers over the fabric while Molly buttoned up the back.

Whether to prove her loyalty to their plan or simply to be helpful, Molly further helped by brushing Casey's long, thick hair and styling the coppery tresses in a loose knot at her nape.

Quinn's knock startled Molly enough to drop an extra pin. "Is there anything else I can do to help?"

"Thank you, no. I appreciate all you've done."

When Casey permitted Quinn's entry, Molly exited at the same time he stepped through the portal into the cozy stateroom. "She didn't finish."

Casey peered down at her stockinged feet. "No, I think I can manage the boots well enough."

"I didn't think to get you new shoes."

Her smile broke through any potential awkwardness. "Such a task requires one to be present for measurements. I'm amazed the dress fits as well as it does. Besides, I prefer my boots."

Quinn prompted her to sit, and against her half-hearted objections, he lifted her left foot onto his knee and guided it into the supple leather. He took his time with the laces before repeating the process with the other boot. "We're not done yet." He went to his saddlebag and removed a thick, white stretch of fabric and unfolded it as he walked toward her.

"I do not need a sling."

"You *do* need a sling."

"I don't."

"You do." Quinn held the fabric open. "I can outlast you. In about five minutes you will have spent whatever energy you had."

Casey presented him with her injured side. "You are insufferable."

"So you keep reminding me." Careful not to agitate her wound, Quinn cradled her bent arm in the makeshift sling, brought the edges around her neck, and tied them off over her opposite shoulder. "How does that feel?"

She gave the full weight of her arm to the sling. Some of the pain dissipated. "Better."

He smiled openly. "You don't have to sound so disappointed." Quinn sat in a chair opposite her. "Before we have to leave these wonderful accommodations in—" he pulled out his watch, "—twenty minutes, let's discuss this list." Quinn presented her with the list of names she started in Silverton.

Casey reached for it and immediately regretted the action. A needle-sharp pain shot through her shoulder. "Where exactly did the bullet enter?"

"An inch to the right of the long scar you have on the back of your shoulder. It didn't go in too deep but enough to cause a lot of bleeding. It missed the bone. You were lucky. By the way, how did you come by the scar?"

"I fell off a horse."

"You fell off."

"Well, not so much fell as tossed. The horse—a male, of course—decided he didn't want to be ridden. I landed on my back on a rock."

"Explains your apprehension at first about riding Paisley. You and she get along well now."

They did, Casey thought. Quite well. Paisley deserves a wide, open pasture with plenty of grass in the summer and a warm place to get out of the snow in winter. Casey pondered what she knew of land for sale outside Denver. She preferred a place far from the city, but she saw so little of her sister now with all the traveling.

"Casey?"

"Hmm?"

"You are miles away."

She moved her eyes until they met his. "Do you ever think about doing something else?"

"Other than lawyering or bounty hunting?"

"Either." She shrugged her good shoulder. "Both."

"Often, which is why I do both. When I grow bored or disillusioned with one, I take up the other." Quinn poured more water for Casey and some for himself before sitting again. "Why do you ask?" He leaned forward and rested his forearms on his legs. "Are you considering a change?"

"I enjoy what I do." She was not yet ready to reveal all the musings of her mind. There would be time enough once they handed off the killer to the authorities. She read the names from the list aloud twice. "Too many suspects and one is as viable as the next. This is going to come down to Molly's identification."

"Perhaps not in the way she expects." Quinn swirled the water in his glass. "Do you trust her? Not in the general sense but this specific circumstance."

"I trust you and Marshal Wickline. I am reserving judgment on everyone else." Casey braced herself as the train slowed for the last mile into Durango. The train chugged and rumbled as it entered the station, and its piercing whistle joined sprays of thick steam as both released into the air and announced their arrival.

Quinn opened the door to the parlor section of the coach and asked Molly to join them. When she entered, Quinn asked, "Are you ready?"

"I am," she said with confidence. "Frightened, I freely admit, but ready."

"You don't have to do this."

Molly glanced at Casey. "I feel I must, to atone for my part in the thefts. I knew deep down it wasn't right, but Levi—"

Quinn held up a hand to stop her. "We understand. All we need from you is to identify anyone you have done business with or may recognize from the mining office."

She bit her lower lip, showing her growing concern. "How am I to do that?"

Casey stood and took hold of Quinn until she steadied. "We

are going to walk into Huckabee Mining Company together. All you have to do is point."

CHAPTER 27

"They'll know it's me!"

"We hope so." Casey held still while Quinn draped her long coat over her shoulders and helped her slip her good arm into a sleeve. The fewer people who noticed her when they walked through town the better. She hoped Miss Mashburn was in good spirits by the time they returned to their rooms at the Strater because Casey wanted a long soak in a hot bath. "We need this person scared enough into confessing, and we have a better chance if he knows we have a witness."

Quinn invited Molly to go ahead of them. He hefted both of their saddlebags over his shoulder and anchored Casey's arm and they followed until Molly stopped before she opened the door to the car's observation platform. "It's time to get off the train Molly."

Her entire body shook in denial. "Not yet."

"Whyever not?" Casey moved past her and looked out the

window. "What is wrong?"

"I see someone who will recognize me. We need to get to the office unnoticed, do we not?"

Casey studied Molly's face for a few seconds. "Preferably. The benefit of surprise will help. Who did you see?"

"A man who's been into the land office a few times. A lot of folks travel between here and Silverton."

Why are you lying, Casey wondered? "Is he still out there?"

Molly shook her head without looking out the window again. Casey and Quinn exchanged a look that conveyed their wariness and waited for Molly to step onto the platform first. Casey held Quinn in place for a minute while the porter assisted their traveling companion. "Where did you put my gun?"

"Casey, your shooting arm is in a sling."

"I can shoot with the other. I may not be as accurate, but I can hit what I aim at."

Quinn lifted the flap on the bag containing her Colt. Instead of handing it to her, he slid it into the deep pocket of her coat. "I'd give you my holster, but you'd draw too many looks when we walk into Huckabee's."

"This will do." Casey patted the outside pocket before slipping her hand in and gripping the familiar handle. "Let's get this over with."

They managed the walk from the station to Huckabee's office without drawing undue attention. Molly stopped half a dozen feet short of the door. "I lied."

"I know." Casey lightly jerked her head at the brick building. "If it has nothing to do with why we're here, then keep your secret. If it does, then tell us now because we will not be forgiving later."

"I sneaked out last night. That's why I wasn't around when you were shot. There's a man—a gentleman—who visits. Levi never knew about him."

"Is this who you saw at the station?" Casey watched for another lie.

Molly nodded. "He must have been on the same train."

"Does he know what you do?" Quinn asked.

"You mean what you hired me to do?" Molly looked around and whispered, "He does. You might know him, being in the same sort of work as some folks he knows."

Casey smiled and meant it. "Well, Molly, we meet all sorts in our line of work, though perhaps not in the way we've led you to think. This will be more interesting than any of us expected." She left the other woman no choice but to enter the building first when Quinn held open the door for them.

Molly looked at Casey over her shoulder. "What do you mean?"

"You will find out soon enough." Regret surged through Casey when she saw Mr. Linwood's desk, knowing the stern-faced secretary would never sit behind it again. In his place sat a young woman who was rifling through the drawers one at a time. The woman blew out a breath and glanced up when

Quinn cleared his throat.

"Pardon me. May I help you?"

Quinn stepped forward, blocking Casey and Molly mostly from the young woman's view. "We're here to see Mr. Huckabee."

"Did you have an appointment? Oh, dear." She swiped loose hair from her face. "Mr. Linwood is away and appears to have taken the diary."

"Inform Mr. Huckabee that Mr. and Mrs. Morgan are here. He will see us." The woman leaned to the left to look around Quinn. He leaned with her. "Please tell him we're here, Miss . . ."

"Nutting. Miranda Nutting."

"Any relation to the mine manager?"

Miss Nutting smiled. "My father! You know him?"

"We have met. At Mr. Huckabee's party."

"I heard it was a grand night. Unfortunately, I was in Denver." She leaned again, this time to the right. "I think I know . . . yes! Molly, whatever are you doing in Durango? Does Percy know you're here?" Miss Nutting rounded the desk, circumvented Quinn, and embraced Molly in a friendly hug. "Did you miss Percy? He said he was going to see you." The woman seemed to have caught on to Molly's intense discomfort. "Are you here with them?"

Molly lost most of the color in her face. "Miranda, you should go. Please tell Percy I will call on him later."

Miss Nutting's glance shifted from one person to the next

and landed on Casey. “I don’t understand.”

“Tell me, Miss Nutting. Do you know a man called Levi Vaine?”

“Of course. He’s my uncle, on my mother’s side. What is going on?”

“A lot more than I anticipated.”

“You know my uncle, as well, then?”

“We have recently made his acquaintance.” Casey used her good arm to motion toward the hallway, then reconsidered. “Have you seen either your brother or uncle today, Miss Nutting?”

“Who did you say you are again?”

Quinn said, “Mr. and Mrs. Morgan. I assure you, Mr. Huckabee will want to see us, and you have yet to answer my wife’s question. It is of the utmost importance we find him.”

Miss Nutting’s hand clasped the front of her throat. “Is he in trouble? Has something happened to him?”

Quinn chose his words carefully. “He is, as far as we know, safe and well.”

“He sent me a telegram this morning to say he’d be staying up north a few days with Molly.” Miss Nutting backed away, though not quickly enough to avoid Casey’s grasp.

Mr. Huckabee’s fortuitous timing saved Casey and Quinn the trouble of getting both Miss Nutting and Molly out of the front office where anyone else could come in.

“Mi—Mrs. Morgan. Mr. Morgan.” He removed his hat and

took in the scene. "You have news for me?" Huckabee glanced at the secretary. "Miss Nutting, you do not look at all well. By the by, what is Percy doing in Durango? He requested a full week."

Casey let go of Miss Nutting in favor of speaking with Huckabee. "Have you seen Percy?"

Huckabee waved his hat over his shoulder. "Not five minutes ago at the stockyard."

"Casey!"

She ignored Quinn's shout as she hurried from the building. "Sir, I must request your help. Do not let Miss Nutting or our guest leave your offices. Lock them in a room and call for the marshal if necessary. We will explain everything when we return."

"Return from where?"

Quinn heard Huckabee's question as the door closed behind him. His long legs carried him across the street in a swift and smooth run. He spotted Casey rush into the stockyard stable. "Damn, stubborn, fool woman!"

The manager quickly got out of Quinn's way as he raced into the stable. His eyes took a second to adjust, and he spotted Raider in a far stall next to the one where Casey attempted to bridle Paisley. "What do you think you're doing!"

"Going after him."

Quinn grabbed the bridle, thwarting Casey's third attempt. He took a moment to soothe the mare. "You can't ride. I'll go. Where did you see him?"

"North."

"Fine." Quinn moved into the next stall and bridled Raider before reaching for the saddle. "If you will go just one day without trying to get yourself killed—" He turned at Paisley's snort and excited whinny in time to see horse and rider emerge from the stall and leave the stable. "I'm going to kill her myself. A slow, agonizing death the likes of which she has never imagined." Foregoing a saddle, Quinn swung onto Raider's back and pursued Casey.

CHAPTER 28

Casey willed the pain away and prayed for continued faith in Paisley. If the horse tossed her about now, she'd break her neck, or worse, break an arm or leg. A broken neck would send her into oblivion. Anything else and she'd be stuck abed for the rest of her natural life.

"Come on, girl. We're nearly there."

The road curved ahead, which is where she lost sight of Percy. She credited him for his horsemanship and upbraided herself for making a mistake. Did he see Molly? Did he figure out Casey's real identity and purpose? Clouds darkened the sky to a deep gray, and the wind stole away the pins securing her hair. Once free, the long tresses whipped in every direction, uncertain where to fly with the wind changing course.

"Casey!"

Quinn's voice reached her scant seconds before she heard the thundering rumble of Raider's hooves pounding over the hard-packed earth. When he came abreast of her, she shouted over the weather. "He's not far ahead!"

"Don't fall off!" Quinn yelled as he and Raider advanced, soon putting three horse lengths between them. He rounded the corner before Casey did, and when she reached the same curve, Percy was nowhere to be seen.

Casey soon realized the greatest error in riding with one good arm—the inability to stop a horse in motion. Quinn brought Raider around and blocked the mare's path, forcing her to halt. Out of breath and dizzy with excitement, Casey asked, "Where do you suppose he went?"

"Do you have any idea what could have happened if were you alone out here and injured? What if the mare had been spooked and you couldn't hold on?"

"I have been in far—"

"Far worse situations, yes, you have been clear about your many escapades. Facing death and danger is another day on the job for you." Quinn's anger seethed on the surface, waiting for an excuse to unleash. "As for Percy, he could be anywhere." He lifted his seat enough to twist and look around. "Except he was not too far ahead of us. When the road straightened, we should have seen him."

"Precisely."

Quinn sent her a withering glance. "What will your sister say when she sees you?"

Casey did not have to think long on the answer. "She will ask if she can come along next time."

"All I need is two crazy women in my life. Ten more minutes and the marshal and his deputy could have joined me instead." He calmed enough to make another careful study of their surroundings. "Over there." Quinn pointed to the mountainside.

"I am not going into another cave."

"You should have weighed the consequences when you set off like a madwoman bent on self-destruction. Look to the left of the cave."

"Ah, a miner's cabin. It appears deserted." Warm liquid seeped down her arm. Casey risked a glance and saw blood drip beneath the sleeve at her wrist. "How angry are you?"

"Angry enough that were I your husband, your backside would be as red as your hair."

"That *is* angry. Of course, you'd never do such a thing, but it tells me I should take care with what I say next."

Quinn held his temper, released a slow exhale, and dared to ask, "Say what?"

She held up her arm for his inspection. Casey expected a curse, a harsh word, or even for him to yank her from the saddle. He did none of those things. Quinn dismounted, tossed Raider's reins over a nearby shrub, and with tremendous care, lifted her off the mare's back. He said not a word as he removed her coat and pulled out his knife.

"Absolutely not."

"I have to get to the wound and redress it before you lose any more blood."

"The blood can be cleaned from the fabric."

"It is only a dress, Casey."

The dress you selected and bought for me. Casey kept the words to herself. "If you unbutton the back partway, you can reach my shoulder. I will not return to town looking like I have tangled with a bear."

Quinn's gaze roamed over her body, from the riotous hair and flushed skin to dust-covered hem. "No one is going to believe you haven't tangled with something." He did as she asked and released enough buttons to reach her shoulder. Two of his meticulous stitches tore. "I can't close this up again out here." He used the knife to lift her top skirt and slice through her petticoat. Folded over, the thick padding stemmed the blood flow. "Hold it there." Quinn cut another strip, this time thinner, and used it to wrap under her arm and over the shoulder four times. He tied it off and re-buttoned her dress. "You'll bleed again if we don't get you back to town."

"No." She continued to cooperate long enough for him to help her back on with the sling and then the coat. "We are too close, and I am weary of the chase." Casey placed her good hand over her heart. "I promise not to die before you have a chance to do the deed yourself."

"I'm going to hold you to that promise." Quinn secured both horses. "I won't waste words asking if you'll stay here, but I will ask if you're okay to walk up there."

Casey figured Quinn got his answer when she stepped across the rocky terrain. The path leading to the modest log cabin was too exposed, so she kept hunched low and behind trees and shrubs until nothing except cold air and space stood between her and the weathered structure. Pain pinched at the wound site, and she adjusted the sling to find a more comfortable position.

A horse's hooves scratched against gravel nearby. She first thought their mounts were agitated by the storm forming above them, but the next time the sound reached her ears, she searched around the cabin. The head of Percy's horse peeked around the corner before disappearing again. His horse appeared again, this time to wander and graze on grass poking up from between rocks and brush.

Quinn tapped her on the shoulder. He pointed to his chest and then to the cabin. She almost disagreed with him until she remembered her promise. Casey held up three fingers to indicate three minutes was all she intended to give him before joining him.

Less than one minute later, Quinn waved her over. He did not enter the cabin through the open door and held out an arm to prevent her from doing so. She quickly saw why.

Casey took the first step inside. "Percy."

The young man's head hung low. He occupied the only chair in the narrow space. She kept her gaze fixed on the revolver he shifted from hand to hand. The older model was not one she recognized, but underestimating a gun was not the concern.

Casey cared only about the man holding it.

Quinn stepped in beside her, his movements measured as he put himself in a position to block her if needed. She appreciated the gesture, even as she hoped it wouldn't be necessary. Casey knew with no doubt in her heart and mind that he would step between her and another bullet.

"Percy. Will you look at me?"

He jerked his head left to right.

"We aren't here to harm you."

"You'll take me back to them. I didn't want to do it. It was an accident."

Casey took one more step closer. "We don't work for them."

Percy raised his head then, and the torment Casey saw in his youthful visage left her quaking. It was a look reserved for those whose agony surpassed their will to live, a flash of hopelessness she had seen only once before in her career and hoped to never witness again. "Percy. You keep the gun if you need to, but will you at least listen?"

"It wasn't supposed to happen." Percy clutched the gun close to him. "He shouldn't have been there."

"Tell us what happened." Quinn's gentle voice helped calm the destructive energy in the cabin. The open door allowed cold air to enter, yet sweat still accumulated on Percy's brow. "Take whatever time you need."

Percy licked away a salty tear that fell on his lips. "Molly told me why you hired her. You're just like them."

Quinn crouched, keeping his back straight and putting himself on a more level position with Percy. In the same move, he also closed the gap between him and Casey. "It was you Molly went out to meet last night, wasn't it?"

Percy nodded. "Will you hurt her?"

What had they done, Casey thought, to bring a man, who by all accounts was not a bad person, to such a devastating point? "Of course not, Percy. We aren't who you think."

His eyes pleaded for more.

Quinn drew him back with his soothing voice. "Our purpose is to reach the end of all of this without any more violence." Quinn held up his hands. "I hold no weapon on you, and neither does she. We need you to meet us partway, to show us that making up for what happened matters to you."

Percy's gaze shifted once more to Casey, who for reasons she could not explain at that moment, approached the younger man and stretched out her hand. "Not for the gun, Percy."

With great trepidation, and likely without thinking it through, Percy accepted her offered hand. Once their palms met, tears fell from his eyes. "Will you betray me?"

Casey believed the only way forward was honesty. "Yes, but not in the way you think. Tell us what happened."

"Mr. Huckabee, Frank, surprised me when I put papers back in his office. He was always real nice. It was only going to be one time, and the Huckabees never needed to find out. That's what they said." Percy held the gun looser now as he focused on the confession he tried to get out. "My pa always said a man has to work for what he gets in this life. He says it like it's easy. No gambling, no whoring, no lying. If a man doesn't do any of those, then he has a chance."

"You paid your debt by helping them, didn't you?" Quinn asked, his focus drifting between Percy's face and the revolver.

Percy nodded. "It was just going to be one time. Just one time."

"What about Mr. Linwood?"

Percy's head dropped again, and he leaned into Casey. Pinpricks of pain shot from the wound site through the rest of her body. She clenched her teeth, closed her eyes, and waited for it to pass. Quinn stepped closer to her, but Casey flashed him a look and a single shake of her head.

Like all the most important decisions in life, Percy had to choose how this moment would end. "Was Linwood involved?"

"No." Percy let go of Casey's hand and sat straighter in the chair. He brought his sleeve across his face to dry the moisture. "He figured it out. What I'd done. Mr. Linwood told me he knew."

"What happened then?" Casey asked.

"They took him away. Levi and a man called Dale. I had nothing against Mr. Linwood, but it all got messed up." Percy gripped the revolver in both hands again. "How did you know about him?"

"We found Mr. Linwood south of Silverton." Quinn

stretched up to his full height and towered once again over the young man. "It wasn't only once, Percy."

"It was!"

Casey tugged on his arm so he looked up at her. "You helped the men who owned your debt come and go. You used the map to mark caves where they could keep what they stole, and you used the locked office. I think what we found there was not meant to be found. You hid it there to use against them." When Percy said nothing, Casey pressed him. "Are we wrong?"

Percy shook his head. "They were going to hurt my sister and father if I didn't cooperate."

"It must have been a significant debt," Quinn said.

The younger man nodded.

"What part did Burton Amos have in all this?" Casey asked.

Percy repeated the name. "Molly's brother?"

Quinn held back his surprise. "You've met him?"

"Not 'til he came here and found me. Said he was here to see his sister. I guess she talked about me." Percy took a deep breath. "He wanted to come up with me to Silverton but he never met me at the station."

Because we sent him away, Casey thought, and good riddance. This meant his attempted attack on Casey was just as Quinn imagined—a disturbed man who saw her about and tried to take something to which he had no right. She did not feel sorry for what he would soon face.

Casey drew Percy's attention back to her. "It's time to tell your story. All of it. Are you strong enough to do that?"

Percy sniffed and wiped his eyes again. "You want to turn me in?"

"I'm a Pinkerton." Casey knew Percy tried to look beyond the wild hair, fancy dress, and arm sling to find the truth of her words. "I don't much look like it now, and that's the idea. I planned to find the person who killed Frank Huckabee and stop at nothing to bring him to justice, even if it meant putting a bullet through him. You are not what I expected, Percy."

"You aren't going to shoot me, then?"

A whisper of a smile crossed her lips for his benefit. "Not if you don't force me. Mr. Morgan asked if you're strong enough to tell your story. Have you decided?"

Neither Quinn nor Casey moved when Percy finally left the chair. His slight frame seemed all the slimmer next to Quinn's height and robust build, and yet, Percy did not cower when he hovered the gun in front of him and gave it to Quinn.

Percy made a fist when he pulled his hand away. "For Mr. Huckabee."

"Not just him, Percy." Quinn passed the weapon to Casey. "You're stronger today than you have ever been, and one day you'll understand why."

CHAPTER 29

The trio sat in Marshal Wickline's office after a slow ride through the first snowstorm of the season. All three needed hot meals to fill their bellies, long baths to ease away aches, and comfortable beds to sleep until the next train rolled through, which by Casey's calculation was too soon.

The marshal listened to Casey's explanation first, as a professional courtesy, he said. His scrutiny of her appearance prompted him to ask if she required a visit from the doctor, to which Quinn promptly said yes before she uttered a denial.

Wickline took up the chair across from Percy but faced Quinn and Casey. "Mr. Huckabee came to me not two hours ago and said I was to lock away two women and not ask questions. I reminded him I work for the people of Durango, not for Huckabee mining."

Casey almost asked if they were the same. "He wouldn't tell you where we went."

"He would not." Wickline wagged a finger at Casey. "I

suspected you might cause me grief, and I was right. But I also owe you—both of you—a great debt. You did what I couldn't."

"Believe me, Marshal, it was more chance than anything else that led us here." Casey offered an encouraging smile to Percy. "Anything you get from now on will be thanks to him."

Marshal Wickline told his deputy to escort Percy to one of the cells behind the jailhouse. Before Percy left the room, he faced Quinn and Casey. "I figure even if I hang, I'll still be grateful for what you did for me out there."

Once they were alone, the marshal asked, "What exactly did you do for him?"

"It has no bearing on the case, Marshal, and isn't our story to tell." Quinn tapped the top of Percy's written confession. "He will need a good lawyer."

"Are you volunteering?"

"There is too much conflict, and I will have to testify, but I have a name, and he owes me a favor."

Wickline scratched his chin. "I've always liked Percy, and his pa and I are good friends, but fact is, he killed a man. And it doesn't matter if someone else murdered Mr. Linwood. They will pay for it, but Percy's actions led to his death, and folks around here won't stand for it. Mr. Huckabee wields a lot of influence from here to Denver."

Casey spoke up. "Percy Nutting is aware of what he's done, and I believe he means to do all he's promised. Mr. Huckabee has the man who killed his brother, and when these thieves are rounded up and brought in, he might even get some of his payroll money back. The Pinkertons have been after these thieves for a long time and won't stop looking until every last one is caught. Molly Vaine will have to answer to the Secret Service for her part in the forgeries, but that isn't our problem."

"Speaking of Molly." Wickline leaned against the table. "Did you mention to Percy the woman he was cavorting with is married to his uncle?"

Quinn smiled at Wickline's furtive peek at Casey. "There probably is not much Miss McKenzie has not already heard."

Casey smiled. "Mr. Morgan is right, and no, we did not tell him. Some matters are far beyond the jurisdiction of the Pinkertons or bounty hunters." When Casey started to rise, Quinn pushed his chair back and helped her stand. "If you will excuse us, Marshal. I have to send word to my supervisor and learn why no one else has arrived."

"About that." Wickline also stood and gathered up Percy's confession. "Workers for the railroad discovered a break in the line two days ago, and they just fixed it yesterday."

Casey thought of the last letter she wrote to Rose that was still waiting to be mailed. At this point, she'd reach Denver at the same time as the mail. "Then I will send word today, and you can expect a lot of guests with badges to arrive soon after."

"Will you be staying in town?"

Casey used Quinn for an anchor as they walked to the door. Her body protested all she'd put it through and longed for a bag of Mrs. Pennyworth's bath salts. "I have other plans. When the trial takes place, it won't be here, not among friends of Frank Huckabee."

"You'll see to it, you mean."

She glanced up at Quinn. "Mr. Morgan might have more sway in that area than I do, but yes. Percy will pay a dear price for what he's done, but he is not beyond rehabilitation."

Wickline scanned the confession. "As for Mr. Linwood killers, I recognize Levi Vaine's name well enough. Poor Miranda. The Nutting family is going to have a hard time of things for a while. Did Percy tell you anything about this Dale person?"

"No, and we will leave it to you to find out." Quinn fixed Casey's sling, still damp, when he noticed the tied knot rubbing against her bare neck. "It is only fair that I tell you it's possible someone advised Mr. Nutting against offering too much information before speaking with a lawyer."

"Sounds like a lawyer already advised him."

Quinn put his hat on and wrapped an arm around Casey's waist. "Not that I recollect. Ellison Huckabee hired me as a bounty hunter."

"Odd how you haven't asked about a bounty."

Casey turned the knob on the door and grinned at Quinn. "How about that."

"Oh, and Mr. Huckabee is demanding to speak with you. Something about your final report and payment."

They ignored Marshal Wickline's parting words, and in the last steps to Casey's hotel room, Quinn lifted her into his arms before she fell asleep standing up.

WATER LAPPED OVER her freshly washed skin, and Casey relished in the steam rising from the copper tub. She cleaned off most of the sweat and dirt from her body, even hampered by her injury. The doctor had examined and restitched the wound at Quinn's insistence, and then ordered Casey not to get it wet for a week.

Her recollection of how she made it from the marshal's offices to the hotel lacked the finer details. When she awakened with the doctor leaning over her, threading a needle through her skin, it was only because of the pressure from Quinn that she did not jump out of bed.

She smiled remembering the doctor's expression, as though he witnessed a woman rising from the dead. He quickly and gently finished his task, wrapped the shoulder with a fresh bandage, and wished Quinn good luck.

Casey did not ask why he thought Quinn needed luck. She raised the sponge over her face and squeezed, relishing in the warm water coursing over her skin. A few light raps at the door interrupted her bliss.

"Casey?"

She barely heard him.

"Just a minute."

Sighing deeply, she got out of the tub and wrapped a towel around her. She found her robe and slipped into it, then glanced at the remaining water. "What a waste." Casey unlocked the door and invited Quinn inside. He quickly closed the door behind him.

"I've just come from Huckabee's office. He made clear his displeasure at not meeting him directly after speaking with the marshal."

Casey used a towel to dry a few escaped tendrils. "Did you tell him he would have our report tomorrow? I have to finish one for the agency."

"He said it was no longer necessary since the marshal filled him in. Durango will be a busy town for the next several weeks. However, our job, other than testifying, is now done. Huckabee asked if we were the ones who disturbed the locked office on the second floor."

Her fingers untangled a section of hair before she secured the strands with another pin. "And what did you tell him?"

Quinn shrugged. "The truth. I also told him what we found there and what it led to, and how his office was used. He is going to close off the hidden staircase and have the office cleaned."

Did she unnecessarily complicate her life? Casey replayed each event from the minute she disembarked in Durango. No, she had to go further back to before Colorado Springs, before Cheyenne, to the beginning of her Pinkerton career. Her uncle would say she enjoyed complications. She could hear her sister saying there was no such thing as a complicated life, just a dull one. Quinn stood next to her when she returned from her musings.

"Here." He handed her four telegrams. "The clerk at the front desk said someone from the telegraph office delivered these all within the last half hour."

She scanned each one and cringed. "Rose threatens to send the calvary if I do not get home soon. Oh, dear. Our mother is coming to Denver."

"Is that a problem?"

"No, but we see her at the holidays. If she is coming home early, it means she is bored, and when Mother has lost interest in all else, she likes to drag Rose and me to all the shops."

"Or she wants to spend time with you. Where is your sling?"

Casey crossed to the bed and held up the fresh cloth the doctor left for her. "I couldn't very well wear it in the bath. What the deuce time is it, anyway?"

"Half-past five. Early for dinner, but I have requested our meals be brought up at six o'clock. I thought you'd want to retire early this evening."

"Hmm." Casey read the telegram from Agent Johnson a second time. "What? Oh, yes, I do."

"Bad news?"

"Not especially. Agent Johnson is pleased with my performance on the case yet vexed with my lack of communication until now." Casey tossed the slip of paper into the wastebin. "He sends a similar telegram after the conclusion of every assignment. I think it is his way of reminding me that he is higher up the chain of command."

"What about the last one?"

"You did not read them?"

Quinn lowered himself into a soft chair. "They were not mine to read."

Pleased with his answer, Casey passed it to him. "Read for yourself."

A few seconds later, Quinn's weary smile changed to a wide grin. "Your sister has a flair for getting her message across. This makes no sense. What does a vase have to do with dead bodies?"

Casey laughed, and it felt good to do so and mean it again. "Her latest investigation. It sounds as though she caught the culprit."

"Much like you."

"Not alone, I didn't. The one beneath it, though, is from my uncle."

Quinn read it three times. "This tells me two things about your uncle. First, he loves you dearly, and second, he is not going to like me. Does he visit Denver often?"

"He rarely leaves Chicago. If he is coming, it is my mother's doing. He can't say no to her."

"Does he ever say no to you?"

Casey grinned. "Not when the matter is important to me."

She pulled back a curtain panel and looked out the window. Fresh snow blanketed the landscape, and thick flakes continued to drift down and cover everything in their path. "Will you walk with me?"

Quinn sat forward. "Do you need help to dress?"

Her lips twitched, but she held back a smile. "I can manage."

"I'll wait in the hall."

Casey saw exhaustion etched across his face; neither of them had enjoyed a full and proper meal in two days. When he passed her, his fingers brushed a loose curl from her shoulder. She stared after his retreating back and wonder what she was supposed to do next.

Fifteen minutes later, wearing a wool dress, her boots, and a long coat, Casey looped her arm through Quinn's. He took the lead and together they walked down the center of the snow-covered road, alone except for the drifting sounds of voices from various points across town.

"Most people are smart enough to stay indoors when nature unleashes the first heavy snow of the season."

Casey leaned her head back and stuck out her tongue to capture a snowflake. "Most people aren't smart enough to enjoy the first heavy snow of the season. Breathe it in, Quinn. Let it fill your lungs. It reminds one to be grateful for each moment we're alive."

"There is much to be grateful for." Quinn guided her in the direction of the train station. "Do you remember the night we met?"

She recalled it fondly. "When you no doubt thought me a harridan. It was not the best of first impressions, running about in my nightclothes as I did."

"You wore your duster." He chuckled when she looked about ready to thrash him. "You suspected everyone, even the drunk imbecile who blew up the wagon. I'm surprised you did not suspect me."

"How do you know I did not?" She gave him a teasing smile. "I *did* suspect everyone, as I too often do. Sometimes a drunk is just a drunk and an idiot merely a nuisance. We have done our good deeds for a while."

"As you often reminded me, you were simply doing your job."

She stopped him in the middle of the road while snow fell and a breeze swirled the flakes around them. "It is never just a job."

"I know."

"It pains me to admit, but I do not believe this would have ended with such success had I worked alone. You saved me, you helped save Percy, and it turns out you are not as infuriating as I first thought."

Quinn brushed snow off her face. "Maybe a little infuriating."

Her lips twisted to prevent a smile. "Maybe a little." She peered over at the train parked for the night, the bold black figure of steel quiet now, but tomorrow it would come to life once again. "Why have you led us here?"

"Two reasons." He smiled. "The first is to settle our wager. The winner can ask any question and the loser must answer."

Casey bit her lower lip to keep from laughing. "It hardly seems fair for you to have to pay up when you worked so hard on the case and even saved my life."

"You believe you won?"

"Certainly, but since I am a fair person, I am willing to call it a draw."

Quinn coughed to mask a chuckle. "How magnanimous you are."

Casey gave up the fight to hold back a deep-throated laugh. "My family is always saying so."

"Hmm." Quinn tilted his head to side to side as he thought that over. "No matter how I imagine it, I do not believe you."

"You are wise man." She laughed again and leaned up on the toes of her boots and pressed a kiss to his cheek. "What is the second reason we are here?"

"It is on there, in the first-class car of that train where I vowed to learn everything about you I possibly could. You ensnared the attention of every man you passed, yet I do not think you noticed a single one."

"Oh, I noticed at least one."

Quinn lifted her left hand and pressed a kiss to it through the supple leather glove. "I should like to meet your sister."

Startled from the tender moment, Casey gaped at him. "You're thinking of my sister?"

"Mm." Quinn maneuvered her into walking again, this time back in the hotel's direction. "You are close with her."

"Of course I am."

"And do you tell each other everything, as close sisters are wont to do?"

"Not everything." Casey tugged the collar of her coat closed. "Most everything."

"And when you introduce me to her, what will you say?"

Even in the darkness, Casey saw a glint in Quinn's hazel eyes. "An incorrigible scoundrel who is far too wise, much too handsome, and who has accomplished the impossible."

This time he stopped, beneath the light filtering from windows above, and turned her to face him. "You think me handsome?"

Casey released a joyful laugh. It came from a place deep within, a place so dark she fretted ever discovering it. "It is time for me to make a change."

Now it was Quinn's turn to be confused by the shift in conversation. "What sort of change?"

"Retirement."

"From investigations?"

"Heavens no. From the Pinkertons. I envy my sister her freedom from restrictions and reprimands."

"You'd be giving up the badge you're so fond of."

She plied his hand open and met his palm to palm. "I will still have my Colt."

"And your blade."

"Both important for getting out of trouble."

"You get into your fair share." He cupped her chin. "Those aren't all you'll have." Quinn lowered his mouth to hers and accepted her breath even as he gave her his. When they parted, it was not to pull away. "Cassandra McKenzie. Will you do me the great honor of taking me with you on your next adventure?"

Casey stood on her toes, wrapped her good arm around his neck, and whispered in his ear, "So long as the adventure will never end."

Thank you for reading

The Case of the Copper King

Don't miss out on future books from MK!

www.mkmcclintock.com/subscribe

Did you know Cassandra's sister, Rose McKenzie, has her own book? Don't miss *The Case of the Peculiar Inheritance* by Samantha St. Claire, another stand-alone novel in the McKenzie Sisters Mystery Series.

ACKNOWLEDGMENTS

My deepest gratitude to all who have helped bring *The Case of the Copper King* into being. To my mother, for your wisdom in giving me and my siblings great childhood memories in Durango. To my wonderful editor, Lorraine Fico-White, for being with me from the beginning and for comments that deserve a blooper reel.

In Durango, to the man who picked up the phone at the Strater Hotel, for answering an important question regarding their elevator, proving the smallest details do matter. I am sorry for not asking your name. To the research team at the Animas Museum, La Plata County Historical Society, for your tremendous help in tracking down a name. To Sharon Greve, local historian and author of *Beyond the Badge 1881-1949*, for your years of unparalleled research.

Considerable thanks to my many generous, amazing, and patient readers. No matter how many times I say, “A new book is finished!” your enthusiasm is humbling. Thank you for the time you spend with my characters in their worlds.

My gratitude, also, to Samantha St. Claire, who invited me to join her on this delightful adventure with the McKenzie sisters. Without you, I would not have met Cassandra and Quinn.